Trial by Fire

A Sanford 3rd Age
Club Mystery

David W. Robinson

Discover us online:
www.crookedcatbooks.com

Join us on facebook:
www.facebook.com/crookedcatbooks

Tweet a photo of yourself holding
this book to **@crookedcatbooks**
and something nice will happen.

About the Author

A Yorkshireman by birth, David Robinson is a retired hypnotherapist and former adult education teacher, now living on the outskirts of Manchester with his wife and crazy Jack Russell called Joe (because he looks like a Joe).

A freelance writer for almost 30 years, he is extensively published, mainly on the web and in small press magazines. His first two novels were published in 2002 and are no longer available. His third novel, The Haunting at Melmerby Manor was published by Virtual Tales (USA) in 2007. He writes in a number of genres, including crime, sci-fi, horror and humour, and all his work has an element of mystery. His alter-ego, Flatcap, looks at the modern world from a cynical, 3rd age perspective, employing various levels of humour from subtle to sledgehammer.

A devout follower of Manchester United, when he is not writing, he enjoys photography, cryptic crosswords, and putting together slideshow trailers and podcast readings from his works.

David's online blog is at: **http://www.dwrob.com**

By the same author

Trial by Fire

A Sanford 3rd Age Club Mystery

Chapter One

Turning into Eastward, the newly promoted Detective Inspector Gemma Craddock wondered how the street had come by such an odd name.

Four thirty on what promised to be another glorious, July morning, and the sun, still below the horizon, would rise on her right, meaning she was driving north, not east. Why call it Eastward? Why not Northward?

She stifled a yawn, her eyes concentrated on the clutch of emergency vehicles up ahead, their blue lights flashing in the dawn.

Eastward was one of those new developments where 'new' meant built within the last five years. The houses were all detached, the lowest price stood at about £200,000, or in other words, completely out of her league. Not that she would want to live here. No sense of community. Gleason Holdings had sold the houses on the back of boasted exclusivity. No single dwelling looked like any other. Bungalow, two and three storey, three bed, four bed, single bed with inverted floors, where the living accommodation stood above bedrooms situated at a lower level. At the far end, where the fire, ambulance and police crews had gathered, stood the dominating spread known as Developer's Dream, a vast and rambling house with an estimated value of about £800,000. It was the home of Gerard Vaughan, the man who had commissioned and built Eastward.

Pulling in behind the Scientific Support van, Gemma yawned again, killed her car engine and mentally corrected herself. It *had been* the home of Gerard Vaughan. What was left of it was uninhabitable.

Once a magnificent, three-storey neo-Georgian mansion, the pristine brickwork was scorched and bulging here and there. Part of the roof had collapsed, either under the heat of the fire or the weight of water from high-pressure hoses. Windows on all three floors were shattered, and pine cladding on the exterior was charred. The brilliant white, uPVC front door, blackened and buckled in places from the heat had been rived from its hinges, and cast to one side, left forlornly on the finely tended lawn, and that lawn itself was scoured and trenched where men and machines (presumably from the Fire Service) had crossed it.

Gemma climbed out of her car to be greeted by PC Vinny Gillespie. Shrouded in a bright lemon, quilt-lined, high-visibility jacket, he appeared grim-faced and tired.

Gillespie had rung at 3:45 and told her they had a body in a fire, and it had been declared a suspicious death. Gemma showered and took a strong cup of coffee. It did nothing to subdue the excitement coursing through her veins.

In a town of 40,000 people, serious crime was rare, and since being promoted to the rank of inspector three months previously, she had investigated nothing more interesting than a robbery at a town centre jewellers. The case had been wrapped up fairly quickly thanks to CCTV footage and her knowledge of the local villains. She had assisted in one or two assault cases in Wakefield, but that aside, life as an inspector was as tame and humdrum as it had been for a sergeant.

And now Gillespie had called her with a murder. Not her first, but the first she would lead. With all due respect to the poor victim, this was just what she needed.

Putting aside the fatigue of a hot summer night and only five hours' sleep, she greeted Gillespie cheerfully. "Morning, Vinny."

"Is it, guv?"

Gemma waved at the gathering light to the east. "So I'm told."

She took in the scene around the house. Three fire appliances were in attendance, their hoses snaking across the ground. An ambulance stood by, its crew of two paramedics drinking coffee from a flask and looking bored. Fire officers moved here and there under the command of their Watch Manager, Bradley Kilburn, and she could see two SOCOs, clad in pale blue overalls and overshoes, going into the house.

She had been told almost nothing over the phone. A fire. A body. Suspicious death. She was duty CID officer for the night. She was needed. As the senior CID officer in Sanford, she would have been needed even if she were not on rota.

Time to draw more information. "All right, Vinny, tell me what we have."

"Brad'll fill you in on the fire side of things, ma'am. I was called out about midnight. They were here when I arrived and I was needed for traffic and pedestrian control." He snorted and waved at the empty street. "Not that we needed it. No one about. Y'know. When Brad and his boys spotted a stiff in the living room, I called the station and asked for the doc. At that point, it was no more than a body in a burning building. Half past three by the time Brad said the building was safe for the doc to go in. He checked the body and called it. Murder. That's when I rang you."

Gemma threw open the boot of her car and pulled out a set of the same pale blue coveralls. Pulling them on, she asked, "Did the doc give you anything more?"

"No, ma'am."

"He still here?"

"Nope. He's shot off back to the mortuary to wait for the stiff."

Pulling the first of her overshoes onto her sensible flats, Gemma tutted. "He should know better. He's supposed to report to me." She pulled on the second overshoe. "Have we ID'd the body?"

"Not officially. Brad reckons its Vaughan, and five'll get you ten he's right. We know Vaughan lives alone."

"Let's not presume anything, eh?"

Gemma closed the boot of her car and made her way

towards the house, ducking under the police crime scene tape. She was met by Kilburn.

"Morning, Gemma. Congratulations on your promotion."

"Thanks." She yawned yet again. "Glad you didn't say 'good morning'. Nothing good about this time of day. Tell me what you know, Brad."

"We were called out about half past eleven last night. Got here, the place was well ablaze. Vinny arrived about half an hour after us, and by then we were tackling it. Had it under control by about one o'clock, and properly damped down by half past two. We saw the body from outside and that's when we went in to check it out. We declared it safe to enter at half past three, and by then we'd done our preliminary." His grimy features took on a more dour appearance. "You're not gonna like this, lass."

"I'm not here to like it, Brad. Just tell me."

"It was deliberate firing and the torch used cooking oil as an accelerant."

Gemma made the connection right away. "You're thinking Uncle Joe?"

Kilburn nodded. "I was there last year, Gemma, when he threatened to kill Gerry Vaughan. After the old Lazy Luncheonette burned down."

"Yeah, but he was only mouthing off. He was angry. Besides, he ended up on the winning side, didn't he? The new Lazy Luncheonette is in the same place as the old one, and he got it cheap for the first two years."

"I'm only saying, Gemma."

"We're gonna need something a lot stronger than cooking oil as an accelerant to pin Joe down."

"And we may have it," Kilburn insisted. "My lads found two pieces in there. A pen and a chef's knife."

"What? They didn't touch them, did they? Only—"

"No they didn't," the fire officer interrupted. "These are experienced fire-fighters, Gemma. In a situation like this, where there's been a death, they know not to touch anything. We left them in situ for your SOCOs to photograph and bag up."

An incandescent blaze of light shone through the missing windows and broken brickwork of the burned out building. Gemma looked through the gaps, and the first crimson arc of the sun's disc forced her to look away again.

Or was it the unnerving idea in her head which forced her to turn away?

"Anyone can buy a kitchen knife, Brad, and most people own pens."

"True," the Watch Manager agreed. "But how many of those kitchen knives have the initials L.M. scratched into the handle. And the pen has an inscription on it. It's a bit burned, but I could make out: 'Thanks from Alec and Julia'. That'll be Alec and Julia Staines, won't it? Big mates with Joe. Members of that club he runs, aren't they?"

"The Sanford 3rd Age Club." Gemma nodded. Drawing in a breath, she asked, "How badly burned is the body?"

"Bad," Kilburn replied. "I've seen worse, mind. I'd guess fifty, sixty per cent. Enough left to identify him, though."

"Definitely Vaughan?"

"After the fun and games he caused with that development on Doncaster Road, anyone could recognise him and, of course, I've had my share of dealings with him on one building or another so I know him as well as I know your Uncle Joe."

Gemma's heart sank. "We've been here before."

"Come again."

She smiled wanly. "The Sanford Valentine Strangler. Uncle Joe was questioned. Wrong. Roy Vickers *accused* him. Joe made us look pretty silly when he cracked it."

Kilburn shrugged. "Your problem, not mine. I'm only reporting to you."

She sighed and called to her colleague. "Vinny. Get the door knocking organised. We need to speak to the neighbours, and I don't give a toss how many of them are still in bed. Knock 'em up."

"Right, ma'am."

Gemma turned back to Kilburn. "Okay, Brad. Let's take a look inside."

***

At just after seven o'clock, a worried Gemma sat with Chief Superintendent Donald Oughton, station commander for Sanford and the surrounding villages.

In his mid to late fifties, Oughton had made it to his exalted rank by the traditional route, starting as a beat bobby in the mid-seventies, and along the way he had done his stints in almost all departments. A tall, slender and a lugubrious man, he was also a friend of Joe Murray. Gemma had the notion they had been at school together.

And she believed it was that friendship which caused Oughton the most concern right now, as he reclined in his executive chair, his pristine white shirt with its black epaulettes and silver adornments gleaming in the morning sun, his gaze concentrated on the view of Gale Street through the windows.

It was not an inspiring prospect. The street was given over largely to local government and law enforcement. The police station took up a large proportion of the street, and then there were the courts, plus a few annexes of the Town Hall, with the odd solicitors' offices here and there. At this time of day, there were few people to be seen. It would get a little busier later, when The Gallery shopping mall, the rear entrance of which was across the street, opened for business, but for the most part, the people to be seen on Gale Street were usually in uniform.

Gemma knew exactly what was going through Oughton's mind and it had nothing to do with the comings and goings outside. After the Valentine fiasco, he would be very wary of pulling Joe in. Small, noisy, irascible, Joe was also astute and possessed with observational powers not granted to mere mortals such as herself and her boss.

And like her boss, she did not believe, for one minute, that Joe had anything to do with events on Eastward.

In an effort to prompt Oughton, she said, "I'm sorry to have dragged you in so early, sir. But Joe is my uncle and I don't want to compromise the investigation."

Oughton stirred as if he had only just realised she was there. "What? Oh. No. That's all right, Gemma. You did the right thing." He smiled encouragement upon her. "You think it's a fit up?"

"I'm certain of it, sir. Joe may be a bad-tempered old bugger, but he's no killer."

"And yet he did threaten Vaughan last year, when the old Lazy Luncheonette burned down. I recall reading your report on the matter."

"He was furious, sir. It was just hot air."

The senior man faced her, and looked down at her interim report on the fire at Eastward. "You have a witness who says he saw a black Ford Ka outside Vaughan's home at eleven o'clock. Half an hour before the Fire Service were called."

"Yes, sir."

Gemma recalled the doorstep interview with Rodney Spencer, an irate, middle-aged man, still wearing his pyjamas and dressing gown, his hair tousled, dentures, missing.

"It was black and like a Volkswagen Beetle. The new one," he had said.

"A Volkswagen. You're sure of that, Mr Spencer?"

"No. I said it was *like* a Volkswagen Beetle, but it wasn't one. It was that Ford thing. The roundy shaped one."

"A Ford Ka?" Gemma had asked, only too well-aware that it was Brad Kilburn's suspicions which led her along that train of thought.

"Yes."

"And you're sure of the colour?"

"No. It was dark, remember. It could have been dark blue or black. All I'm saying is…"

Oughton's voice broke into Gemma's recollections. "What does Joe drive? A Vauxhall, isn't it?"

Her increasing anxiety forced Gemma to swallow hard. "No, sir. The Vauxhall went up in smoke with the original Lazy Luncheonette."

"So what is he running now?"

"A Ford Ka. A black Ford Ka."

Oughton looked up sharply. "Oh, that's it, then. We have to bring him in."

"Yes, sir, I thought we would have to. But…"

Gemma trailed off. She did not want to put into words what was going through her mind. On the one hand she was concerned for her uncle. Joe had a reputation for being abrupt to the point of rudeness, but by and large, he was a respected member of the Sanford community, and a man who believed in the rule of law. Her father, who had also been a policeman, and her mother, sister to Joe's ex-wife, had been firm friends with Joe ever since Gemma could remember, and the little caterer had done as much as her father to encourage her when she first joined the police.

Behind her concern for her uncle, however, there was a good deal of anger. This was the first serious crime where she had the opportunity to lead the investigation and demonstrate her abilities, yet she knew that Oughton would not permit it.

Her boss confirmed it. "I'm sorry, Gemma, but I can't let you handle it."

From a purely practical point of view, it was the correct course of action. Although Gemma (and Joe) would insist that she was impartial, the press and the public were hardly likely to see it in the same light, and in small town like Sanford, it would not take long for the public to learn that one of its best-known traders was the subject of an investigation led by his niece.

"Sir, I…"

Oughton held up his hand for silence. "We have a *prima facie* case of murder on our hands, and we're only waiting for forensic and pathology reports to confirm it. Rightly or wrongly, we don't always enjoy the best of reputations. I've no doubts that Joe is innocent, but I cannot allow you to run an investigation into such a serious crime where he's implicated."

Gemma suppressed her disappointment. "Who, then, sir?"

The Chief Superintendent drummed his fingers on the desktop. "By rights, I should ring Wakefield and ask for Chief Inspector Vickers, but we know what happened last time."

Joe had been implicated in the case of the Sanford Valentine Strangler, and Vickers had made life more than uncomfortable for her uncle.

"He has a downer on Uncle Joe, sir."

"Correct, and your uncle went on to make us all look like amateurs. But the evidence then was largely circumstantial. This—" Oughton gestured at her report "—is probably circumstantial, too, but it's a little more concrete. The car is what swings it for me."

"Yes, sir."

He leaned back in his chair again, this time concentrating his steady gaze on the ceiling, and Gemma could almost hear his mind ticking over the possibilities.

She sneaked a glance at her watch and read 7:15. At The Lazy Luncheonette, Joe would be in the deepest throes of his morning rush and he would not be pleased to see her, let alone any other police officer. And yet, she was certain all she needed was ten minutes of his time to clear up the matter and get the *real* investigation under way.

"I think I'll call Ray Dockerty in Leeds."

She nodded. "I've met Chief Inspector Dockerty before, sir."

"It's Superintendent Dockerty, these days."

"Yes, sir. Unfortunately, I think Joe's met him, too."

Oughton nodded sagely. "Christmas a couple of years back. That nasty bit of business at the Regency Hotel in Leeds. Wasn't one of Joe's pals initially accused?"

"George Robson, if memory serves, sir."

Oughton chuckled. "Big George. He was one of Joe's gang at school, you know. They terrorised the schoolyard." He laughed again at his memories. "And they're still friends."

"George is a member of Uncle Joe's club."

"The Sanford 3rd Age Club? I'm a member, too...

technically. Haven't been to one of their shindigs for years." Her boss peered over the thin rims of his varifocals. "Because of our association with Joe, neither you nor I are qualified to investigate this matter, Gemma. We need someone who is as fair minded and impartial as he can be. I don't know all the ins and outs of the Leeds case, but I know Ray quite well. He's more than capable of putting aside any personal feelings he may have towards your uncle. And if the waters are to be muddied, we may find we need a superintendent on the case, rather than an inspector or chief inspector. I'll have a word with him."

Gemma sucked in her breath. "Very good, sir. Is there anything you want me to do now?"

"Yes. Cut along to The Lazy Luncheonette and bring Joe in."

"But sir, could we not—"

"No, you cannot conduct the interview on his premises. I've already made it clear that you cannot interview him at all. He's implicated. We need him here for a formal interview with officers who are independent of this station, this *town*. Bring him in. Give him only the barest of information, and before you do that, ask if he can account for his whereabouts between, say, half past ten and midnight last night. You do not tell him why, and you don't give him the opportunity to cook anything up with Brenda Jump."

Gemma got to her feet. "I don't think he and Brenda are an item these days, sir."

Chapter Two

It was often said the Joe Murray only had two moods: bad and very bad. Like many of the myths concerning Joe, there was more than an element of truth in it. Most days he was simply irritable, but it would not take much to elevate him to a plateau of real anger.

Crawling out of bed at a quarter to five, climbing into his car for the two-mile journey to The Lazy Luncheonette, was calculated to raise any sane person's blood pressure, but realising that he had not filled the car (he was sure he had more petrol than that) meant a detour to the all-night filling station on North Road, and that was enough to tip the scales.

"The tank on this thing is so small you only need to go to the supermarket and back and you're out of juice," he complained to his nephew Lee when they finally got the gas burners lit in the kitchen.

Turning up late created problems of its own when running a truckers' café. They would be busy from the moment they opened the doors at six, and it would be impossible to catch up.

"We've already lost at least two customers," he whined as he waited for the tea urn to come to the boil.

"How d'you work that out, Uncle Joe?" Lee asked as he spread cooking oil and laid out multiple rashers of bacon on the flat span of the cooking hob.

"There were two truckers parked overnight in the back lane last night. They've already gone. That's two breakfasts we're down."

Pouring more oil from a 20-litre metal drum into the deep fat fryer, Lee pointed out, "Yeah, but they could have gone really early doors. Y'know, like four o'clock or whenever. Anyroad, how come you saw them?"

"I went to the cash and carry after we closed last night, picked up a load of perishables. I didn't want all those cakes and buns and the frozen stuff in the car overnight, so I called back here and dropped them off." Joe checked a line of photographs on the wall. "Remember, lad, all of this, including journeys to the cash and carry, will be yours one day... well, most of it. Apart from the bits I leave to Sheila and Brenda."

The centre picture was of himself, Sheila Riley and Brenda Jump standing alongside his car at the rear of The Lazy Luncheonette. Taken by Lee back in December, when they first moved in, all three wore broad smiles. Alongside it was a photograph of Lee standing at the front entrance, and next to that was another of Sheila and Brenda, then another of Joe, but his smile in this image was faded. It irritated him that the new building had no parking out front, and he could not have his picture taken alongside his car in front of the café.

"My two prized possessions," he muttered and flicked over the pictures with a feather duster.

"What, Uncle Joe?"

"Nothing, Lee. I was just thinking about the café and my car. Just talking to myself. And we'd better get a move on. The girls will be here soon, and the draymen won't be far behind them."

Busy unlocking the door, Joe did not bother to check if Lee had heard or responded to the instruction. For all that he was the butt of Joe's irritation much of the time, Lee was diligent and knew exactly what he was supposed to be doing.

Although Joe described Lee as a 'lad' he was in fact almost thirty years old. Often clumsy, sometimes slow on the uptake, he had been a professional rugby player, a useful prop for the Sanford Bulls until torn knee ligaments ended his career. He was born in Sanford, but his father, Joe's brother Arthur, had moved the family to Australia when Lee

14

was a toddler. Less than five years later, Arthur's wife, Rachel, returned to England with young Lee in tow, and Joe had become a surrogate father to the boy, ensuring that he went to school and later, when he turned sixteen, unwilling to let him rely on playing rugby for his income, he had sent Lee to catering college. A huge, often cumbersome young man, he was nevertheless an excellent chef, quite capable of turning out the kind of fancy meals The Lazy Luncheonette did not sell. Joe had warded off the threat of some fancy restaurant or hotel chain stealing Lee away by bequeathing eighty per cent of the café to him. The other twenty per cent would go to Sheila and Brenda who, as well as working for him were, coincidentally, his best friends.

They arrived on the dot at seven, at which time there were half a dozen truckers enjoying breakfast in the dining area.

Putting on a tabard from a locker in the kitchen, Brenda ran a practised eye over the food preparation area. "Are we a little behind?"

Joe glanced at her and ran a cynical eye down to her legs. "You don't look too bad, Brenda. For your age."

"One of these days, Joe, you'll get a knuckle butty for breakfast. I asked are we a little behind, not have we a little behind."

"I was late," Joe told her, "and it was your fault."

"How come?" Sheila wanted to know as she checked the empty tables for sugar, salt and pepper. "Brenda, did you stay with Joe last night?"

"I did not."

"No, but you went out with the sandwich order yesterday morning," Joe said, "and you never told me how short of petrol I was. I had to detour this morning to fill the car up."

"Can't say I noticed," Brenda replied as she strapped on an apron and began to help Lee in the kitchen.

"We won't have enough sausages cooked for the draymen, Uncle Joe," Lee called out. "They'll have to wait."

Joe looked to the door where the first of the Sanford

Brewery delivery drivers stepped in with his mate in tow. "I can see this being a fun day."

By half past seven, the queue still stretched back to the door, as it usually did, but the drivers were becoming more vociferous in their complaints.

"Every pub in Sanford will be out of ale by the time we get moving," complained the drayman at the front of the queue.

"You want uncooked bacon? It takes time. We can't cook it any faster."

"Yeah but—"

"Or maybe you think it'll cook a bit quicker if it's marinated in Sanford Brewery best bitter. Gimme a couple of barrels and we'll try it."

It was into this chaos that a tired Gemma and Vinny Gillespie entered at seven forty-five.

"I don't know what you want, Gemma, but you'll have to wait," her uncle said. "We're miles behind. I'll sort you some tea out."

"I don't have time for tea, Uncle Joe, and we can't wait. Get your whites off. You have to come with us to the station."

The announcement brought silence to the entire place. Draymen, usually engrossed in their work-related chitchat, or the latest, closed-season football transfer news, stopped, and bent their ears to events at the counter. Busy clearing a few tables Sheila, too, stopped, and in the open-plan kitchen, both Lee and Brenda paused to listen in.

"Just mind your own business and get on with your meals," Gillespie ordered everyone.

No one took any notice.

Joe glowered. "Have you taken leave of your senses, girl? I'm in the middle of the morning rush."

"Uncle Joe, I've had a long night, and Vinny's been on duty longer than me. You're needed at the station for questioning."

"Questioning? What about?"

Joe could make out Sheila mouthing 'about what' but for

once, she did not say it aloud.

"I'm not prepared to discuss it here," Gemma replied.

"Fair enough. Then I'm not coming with you."

"Uncle Joe—"

"Gemma, don't try to pull the wool over my eyes. If you need to question me over something, I have the right to know what."

She sighed. "I'm not prepared to discuss it here," she repeated, "but let's say it's a serious incident."

"How serious?"

"It doesn't come much worse." Gemma held his gaze. "If you don't come with us voluntarily, you'll leave me no choice but to arrest you."

Joe gawped, and then the anger took over. "Oh, it's like that is it?"

The drayman waiting for service grinned. "You been dumping chip fat down the drains again, Joe?"

"Bugger off, you."

"Not until I've been served."

Blatantly ignoring his niece, Joe poised his pen over a note. "Whaddya want?"

"Joe, this is your last warning," Gemma said. "You are coming to the station. Now."

In the kitchen, Brenda and Lee were talking earnestly. Lee broke off the conversation and stepped across to pick up the wall phone. "You'd better go, Uncle Joe. I'll bell Cheryl. She'll be here in twenty minutes."

"I'm going nowhere until I'm told what it is."

"I'll tell you in the car," Gemma insisted.

Sheila returned to the counter. "Joe, go with her. Whatever it is, I'm sure it'll be sorted out quickly. We can cope until Cheryl gets here."

Joe ignored her. "What's it about, Gemma?"

"That's it." Gemma finally snapped." Joseph Murray, I'm arresting you on suspicion of murder. You do not have to say anything, but it may harm your defence if you fail to mention when questioned something which you intend to rely on in court. Anything you say may be given in evidence."

For the second time, complete, stunned silence fell over the busy café. Behind the counter, Joe's hand began to shake and the colour drained from his face.

Alongside Gemma, Gillespie unclipped his handcuffs.

"I don't think we'll need them, Vinny," Gemma said.

Joe removed his whites, hung them up. After putting on a thin gilet, he fell in between his niece and her colleague, and under the watchful eyes of everyone in the café, walked out with them.

At the kerbside, Vinny watched him into the rear seat of their patrol car before getting behind the wheel. Gemma climbed into the passenger side, and ordered, "Gale Street, Vinny."

Joe spoke for the first time as Gillespie pulled away into the traffic. "Are you gonna tell me what this is about?"

"I can't. I'm not allowed."

"Don't talk so soft, woman."

"I'm under orders, Joe. You are my uncle. You're suspected of murder. I cannot speak to you about it."

Joe turned to the driver. "Vinny—"

"I can't either, Mr Murray. We've known each other too long."

"Just sit tight and wait," Gemma ordered. "Someone will be speaking to you sooner rather than later."

"I haven't done anything."

"Then you've nothing to worry about, have you?"

***

When Gemma entered Chief Superintendent Oughton's office for the second time, it was to find two other men with her boss.

She remembered Detective Superintendent Raymond Dockerty as a man able to command others by his very size.

An old-fashioned copper who, like Oughton, had come up through the ranks, he was tall, bulky, square shouldered, with dark hair thinning on the crown, and had fists the size of hams, and when he spoke it was with a loud, booming voice which demanded attention. He enjoyed an enviable arrest record and a reputation for thoroughness, and the rumour factory had it that the only reason he had not made superintendent earlier was his absolute refusal to bend to his superiors' will, coupled to a habit of telling it like it was, regardless of whose delicate ears his words fell upon.

By contrast, Detective Sergeant Issac Barrett was a university graduate who had been fast-tracked into CID. Wearing an expensive suit, he was younger than Gemma but had risen through the ranks so much faster. Not that she was fooled by his prim appearance, or his soft-skinned, finely manicured hands. Working under a man like Dockerty, he would have to be the best.

Oughton waved her into the only remaining seat, and said, "I believe you know Superintendent Dockerty and Sergeant Barrett."

She nodded a brief greeting to the two men. "We've met before, sir, at training sessions in Leeds and Wakefield."

"I remember," Dockerty replied. "And congratulations on your recent promotion."

"Thank you, sir."

Oughton reclined in his seat and allowed Dockerty to take control.

"We're as short of manpower in Leeds as you are here, but I have the advantage of two Chief Inspectors who can hold the fort while I'm here, so I decided to take on this case myself. Now, I've read your initial report and although all the evidence is largely circumstantial, it clearly points at Joe Murray. He's your uncle on your mother's side, isn't he?"

"Slightly more complicated, sir," Gemma explained. "His ex-wife is my mother's sister. He was also a great friend of my father, who was one of Sanford's best-known community constables, and latterly a uniformed sergeant. Between them Joe and my dad persuaded me that the police service was the best career I could choose."

Dockerty had allowed her to speak even though she got

the impression that he felt she was overegging the pudding.

"You're close?"

"I wouldn't say close, but I do see a lot of Joe, and of course, as family, we keep in touch socially."

"In that case, you cannot be permitted to take any active part in the investigation while he's a suspect."

"I understand that, sir." While she spoke Gemma cast a rapid glance at Oughton, who seemed more interested in the street than their debate.

Dockerty obviously noticed. "Chief Superintendent Oughton is under the same restriction. He and Joe are friends, too."

Gemma said nothing.

"While we were on our way over from Leeds, Sergeant Barrett brought me up to speed on the last time Joe was suspected of murder. The serial stranglings, known as the Sanford Valentine Strangler killings. Chief Inspector Vickers led that investigation, and he treated Joe pretty poorly, didn't he?"

"Frank opinion, sir? The answer is yes. Mr Vickers bullied Joe on the strength of circumstantial evidence which wasn't as strong as what we have now. The chief inspector then went on TV and to the local media to announce that Joe had been arrested. He also refused to listen to me when I had material evidence which cast doubt on the whole case. If Chief Superintendent Oughton hadn't intervened, the strangler could still be free."

"Joe had embarrassed him previously. Or so I'm told."

"Yes, sir. But Joe's like that. Grumpy, snarky, narky, he goes on as if he's the only one who has the brains to deal with anything and everything. It's just his way."

Dockerty nodded. "You're aware that Joe and I have had prior dealings?"

"The Regency Hotel business a couple of Christmases back."

"Joe pulled exactly the same stunt on me as he did Vickers." Dockerty leaned forward. "But there's a difference, Gemma. I don't bear grudges. None of us should. We have a job to do and we can't do it if we allow personal preference or prejudice to get in the way. That's why I can't allow you on this investigation." He indicated Barrett with a nod. "Ike will act as my bagman. You will confine yourself to your other cases and if you're free, you will work with the DCs and the uniformed staff in the collation of statements and evidence, but you will never work alone on them. Do you understand?"

Gemma felt her anger rising again. "Yes, sir. However, I do feel that pratting about with statements and evidence is demeaning for a detective inspector. It's the kind of work we usually give to juniors and probationers."

Dockerty had his large hands apart, accepting her criticism. "You're right, but what can I do? Don – Chief Superintendent Oughton, can't afford to lay you off, and I can't afford to have you involved in this investigation. Even going out to bring Joe in is chancy."

"If you say so, sir."

"I do." Dockerty's tone brooked no further argument. "However, you have my personal assurance that Joe will be given every opportunity to demonstrate his innocence and the very moment I'm happy that he's no longer a suspect, he will be freed, and you will then come into the investigation as my 2IC."

Gemma felt slightly mollified. She had no doubts about Joe's innocence, and with luck, she would be in on the case within twenty-four hours.

"Now, have you told him anything?"

Again Gemma glanced at Oughton. "No, sir. I was ordered not to."

"Did he come along willingly?"

"No, sir. He was in the middle of his busiest time and he kicked up a stink." She swallowed a lump in her throat. "I had to arrest him."

"Painful for you, and I'm sorry, but you did the right thing. Where is he now?"

Gemma made a conscious effort to bring her emotions under control. Feeling sorry for herself or for Joe would not get her any further. "Interview room two. Constable Wickes is with him. He's, er, not in co-operative mood, sir."

"Leave that to me." Dockerty stood. "Don, I'll get on with it."

"Fine, Ray," Oughton replied with an apologetic glance at Gemma.

Chapter Three

Joe, with Constable Noel Wickes babysitting him, was pacing the interview room when Dockerty and Barrett arrived.

Over an hour had passed since Gemma booked him in. He had refused to call his solicitor, after which he was left in this tiny room with only the uncommunicative Wickes for company. He had been told nothing, other than he was suspected of murder. While recognising the seriousness of the matter, he was innocent, and as far as he was concerned, he should be behind his counter at The Lazy Luncheonette, and any questions the police may have should have waited until mid-morning when it would be easier for him to leave his business.

He was doubly annoyed with Gemma. She was his niece. With a few exceptions, no one in Sanford knew him better. She knew he was no criminal, and she also knew how The Lazy Luncheonette worked. Beyond anyone in this station, she should have understood his need to be back there, running his business, not left to simmer in this stuffy, windowless, eight by eight, room. She had her duty, and he would not criticise her for carrying it out, but duty did not mean absolute, obdurate inflexibility.

So he passed the hour alternately sitting and fulminating over the situation, and pacing the tiny room in an effort to calm his growing frustration.

By the time Dockerty and Barrett entered just after nine o'clock, he was almost rabid, but while the two detectives dismissed their uniformed colleague, Joe subdued his anger, and put a broad, cynical smile on his face.

"Well, well, well. Sanford's finest can't cut it; Roy

Vickers is still scared of me so they send for the big guns from Leeds. Chief Inspector Dockerty and Constable Barrett."

Putting down two evidence bags, while Barrett spread a statement form on the table and began labelling cassette tapes, Dockerty took his seat, set a buff folder in front of himself, and only then responded to Joe. "It's Superintendent Dockerty now, Mr Murray. And Issac is a sergeant."

"I'll bet you won those promotions after I cracked the Regency Hotel case for you." Joe's light-hearted jibes hid his fury at the position he found himself in, and it was obvious from Dockerty's bland stare that they knew it.

"Before I start the tape, what have you been told about this morning?"

"That I've been arrested, by my own niece, on suspicion of murder. It's—"

Dockerty cut him off. "I must apologise for that, Mr Murray. Because of your relationship to her, Detective Inspector Craddock should not have been sent. However, as I understand it from Chief Superintendent Oughton, this station is desperately short of manpower, so he had little choice."

Joe opened his mouth to protest, but Dockerty got in first.

"I also understand, from Inspector Craddock's verbal report, that the reason she arrested you was because you would not come along voluntarily."

Joe let rip, venting the volcanic anger of the entire morning in a loud and razor-edged diatribe. "And why? Because I'm not like the usual dole fodder you get in here. I'm a businessman. That means I have a business to run and your lot turned up right in the middle of the busiest time of day. Could it not have waited for a few hours?"

"It's a murder investigation, sir," Barrett pointed out.

"Yes, and I'm not guilty."

"That remains to be seen," Dockerty said. "We have a lot to get through, Joe, and we'll get through it quicker if you keep your temper under control and answer the questions factually. No stupid rants about your innocence or police stubbornness. When we're done, as long as I'm happy that you're not implicated or that we cannot demonstrate your involvement, you will be free to go back to your business. Are we clear on that?"

There was much Joe wanted to say, but the sense of Dockerty's words seeped into his brain and lodged themselves there. How many times had he advised others to co-operate with the police? How many times had he made a firm effort to calm someone down and encourage them to co-operate with the police? It was the simplest, quickest way to having the charges dismissed.

"Yes." Unwilling to let matters go with a monosyllabic reply, he added, "I don't even know who I'm supposed to have killed."

"Gerard Vaughan," Dockerty replied.

The shock stunned Joe momentarily. Mental images dashed through his mind in lightning succession, so fast that they ran like a silent movie produced on a hand-cranked camera. Meetings with Vaughan and Irwin Queenan, The Lazy Luncheonette burned to the ground, the temporary accommodation on the industrial estate opposite, moving into the brand new place, Vaughan's anger at being outmanoeuvred, his ensuing arguments with Joe, the blazing confrontation between them in front of the old, ruined café on the morning after the fire.

He brought his teeming thoughts under control. "Vaughan?"

Dockerty nodded but said nothing. Instead, he watched Barrett setting up the recorder.

"But... I, er..."

The superintendent held up a finger for silence until Barrett gave him the nod, at which point he spoke directly at the recorder.

"Interview number one on the suspicious death of Gerard Vaughan. Present are myself, Detective Superintendent Raymond Dockerty, Leeds CID." He nodded at Barrett.

"Detective Sergeant Issac Barrett, Leeds CID."

Dockerty now faced Joe. "Please identify yourself for the recording, sir."

"Joe Murray, The Lazy Luncheonette, Doncaster Road, Sanford."

"Your full name, sir, and your home address, not your place of business," Barrett said after checking Joe's details taken as he had been booked in.

Joe grunted. "Joseph Murray, Flat twenty-one, Queen's Court, Leeds Road Estate, Sanford."

"Thank you, Mr Murray," Dockerty said. "Can you confirm that you have been advised of your right to have legal representative present during this interview, and you have declined."

"I have *reserved* the right," Joe corrected him. "I'm not paying some legal mouthpiece a coupla hundred pounds an hour to say what I can say myself, but if you get too stroppy, I'll call him."

"Very well. How much have you been told about the incident?"

"Nothing. I wasn't even told who I'm supposed to have murdered until just now."

"In that case, sir, I will run through the events as they were reported, and from there I will go on to question you. Okay?"

Joe nodded. "As you wish."

Dockerty drew Gemma's initial report before him and spent a moment studying it, before beginning the account.

"At eleven thirty last night, the Fire Service, under the command of Yellow Watch Manager Bradley Kilburn, were called to a property identified as Developer's Dream, on Eastward, here in Sanford. When they arrived they found the property well alight, and it was one thirty in the morning before they had the blaze under control. Another forty-five minutes passed before Mr Kilburn could enter the building. On entering, he and several of his crew found the body of Gerard Vaughan in what was left of the living room. The body has not yet been formally identified, and it was badly burned, but Kilburn said that what remained of the face was sufficient to recognise Vaughan, whom he knew."

"Most of Sanford knew him." Joe was unable to keep the contempt out of his voice.

Registering only the slightest of frowns at the interruption, Dockerty went on.

"Mr Kilburn's initial report indicates that the fire was started deliberately, and although it's too early to be absolutely certain, he indicates that petrol was used to start it, and cooking oil was spread around the place as an accelerant."

Dockerty waited to see if Joe would say anything. Joe maintained a bland stare and remained silent.

"The fire crew found several pieces of physical evidence on the floor of the house, including two items which are of particular interest to us. However, we will come to those in a few moments. The police, including Scientific Support and the medical examiner, were called and arrived on the scene at about three a.m. it was almost three thirty before the building was declared safe for them to enter. The medical examiner indicated that the body had suffered a deep knife wound to the heart. It's too early to say whether this was before or after death, but logic would seem to dictate that it was the cause of death."

"If it had been post mortem, the idiot killer would have had to stay in a blazing building, wearing breathing apparatus before knifing him," Joe cut in, demonstrating that his anger had not robbed him of his logical capabilities.

"Precisely." Again, Dockerty frowned. "We are waiting for a full post mortem report, but it's likely to be a day or two before we get it." He checked the report again. "After photographing the scene and evidence in situ, scene of crime officers removed several pieces from the house. At just before five a.m. the police started house to house inquiries with the neighbours, and one, a Mr Rodney Spencer, of 39, Eastward, which is approximately one hundred yards from the scene, reported seeing a dark-coloured Ford Ka arrive at the house at about eleven p.m. half an hour before the Fire Service were called."

Dockerty pushed the report to one side, and sat back, his arm resting casually over the back corner of his chair.

"Now, Mr Murray, can you confirm that you know Gerard Vaughan?"

"Yes. He burned down my old café."

In the first real show of irritation, Dockerty tutted. "For the benefit of the tape, although he was questioned, there is no evidence that Mr Vaughan was involved in the fire at the original Lazy Luncheonette on Doncaster Road."

"He didn't do it personally, man," Joe protested. "His sort never do. He paid someone to do it."

His anger growing, Dockerty nodded at the recorder.

"Interview suspended at nine twenty-three," Barrett said into the machine.

Dockerty rounded on his suspect. "Joe, I asked you not to start losing it."

"Yes but—"

"Remember, I know next to nothing about Sanford, and even less about Vaughan. I don't care if he paid the baker to star the Great Fire of London. He has been murdered. Whether or not he deserved it is not for any of us to say. It is a crime and that is what I'm investigating. We'll make more progress if we can stick to the matter in hand all right?"

Joe acquiesced in silence, and Dockerty nodded again to Barrett, who restarted the machine. "Interview recommenced at nine twenty-five."

"Right, Mr Murray, you have confirmed that you knew the deceased." Dockerty laid a gimlet eye on Joe. "Would it be fair to say you had an antagonistic relationship with him?"

In the light of Dockerty's last outburst, Joe kept his answer simple. "Yes."

Dockerty rummaged through the folder, until he found what he was looking for. "I have here a report, made again by Detective Inspector Craddock, on an altercation outside the original Lazy Luncheonette, on the morning after it burned down. In that report, Inspector Craddock indicates that you uttered threats against Mr Vaughan. Is that correct?"

Joe could not hold back this time. "Oh, come on. I was livid. Losing the plot. It was hot air."

Dockerty checked the report again. "According to Inspector Craddock, your precise words were, 'I'll kill you, Vaughan. Just let me get my hands on you'. Would you agree with that?"

"I can't remember."

"But you were angry?" Barrett asked.

"I just said so, didn't I?"

When neither man responded, Joe went on the defensive.

"Look at me, for God's sake. Do I look as if I'm big enough, or even young enough to take a man like Vaughan on? Ask any of my friends. I'm not a scrapper, let alone a murderer."

While Barrett made hurried notes, Dockerty replaced the report in the folder. "Let's put that to one side a moment, and come to last night. Can you tell me where you were between, say, ten thirty and eleven thirty?"

"At home in bed. I have to be up at half past four every morning."

"Can anyone confirm that?"

"No. I live alone."

"You do own a dark-coloured Ford Ka, don't you?" Barrett asked.

"Yes. It's black. I bought it after the old place burned down." Joe took in Barrett's blank stare, and scowled back. "I had no choice. My old car got caught in the fire and it was a wreck."

"You didn't loan your present vehicle to anyone last night?" Barrett asked.

"No. I parked up at about half past seven, and at five this morning, the car was right there, where I'd left it. It never moved."

Obviously goaded by Joe's certainty, Barrett retorted, "We have a witness who says different."

"According to him," Joe said, pointing at Dockerty, "your witness only described a dark-coloured Ford Ka. You

29

think I'm the only man in Sanford who owns one?"

"All right, all right." Dockerty reasserted his control. "Sergeant Barrett, you were out of order there and Mr Murray is right. Without further evidence, we cannot presume the car seen on Eastward is his."

"Yes, sir." Barrett, appearing suitably contrite, addressed Joe. "My apologies, Mr Murray."

"No harm done, son."

Dockerty brought the interview back on track. "Let's concentrate on other matters. Although we're waiting for verification from both specialist fire officers and our own forensics services, the early indications are that cooking oil was used as an accelerant. You run a popular café and I imagine that you use a lot of cooking oil."

"Gallons of it," Joe agreed. "It comes in twenty-litre metal drums and I have them delivered five drums at a time." He leaned forward, jabbing his finger into the table top. "But I keep accurate records and I can account for every drum."

"Even those you've used?" Barrett's disbelief resounded in his voice.

"As it happens, yes. They're metal drums, and I store the empties in a purpose-built recycling shed out the back of the café. Along with cardboard boxes and other, recyclable materials. Now and again, a lad comes along and takes the drums away. He gives me a few quid apiece for them. I don't know whether they go for scrap or they're cleaned up and re-used by the industry, but I do know it's a kosher arrangement. It's not a backhander. The lad gives me a receipt for the exact number of drums he takes. I have all those receipts and I have invoices which account for the full drums I still have on the premises, and everything goes through my books. If you add up the empties I've let go, and those that I have in the shed, plus the full ones in the café, you'll find they all tally. There is not a single drum unaccounted for."

"That's as may be," Dockerty said, "but it's irrelevant."

Joe's eyebrows rose. "Irrelevant?"

"If memory serves, there's a wholesale warehouse type place on Sanford Retail Park, right behind your café. The kind of place where you have to be a member to shop. You could have gone there and bought another drum for cash. Or you could have bought one on the internet, for example."

"Go and ask them. Check my credit card details. You'll have to come up with something better than that, Dockerty."

The Superintendent gave the matter a moment's thought. "Okay. Let me paint a picture for you. For the moment, let's assume you did this. You went along to Vaughan's house last night, carrying a drum from your café because you fully intended to kill him. After doing so, you then set fire to the house by spreading a little petrol on the floor, then splashed cooking oil all over the place and torched it. You brought the drum out with you, put it in the boot of your car, and then, when you arrived for work this morning, you dropped it into the empty store along with other empties. That would produce absolutely no discrepancy in your figures."

Joe considered it for a moment. "But it would produce images on the building's CCTV."

Now it was the turn of the detectives to be surprised. "CCTV?" Barrett asked.

"This new building is largely offices. Some window fronts on the ground floor along with my place. An estate agents, solicitors, that kind of thing. No one keeps any serious cash lying around, not even me, but there's a lot of expensive machinery in those offices. There's CCTV coverage at each end of the building front and rear, and there's a permanent security officer on duty. He monitors both the inside and outside of the building. He'd have me on tape arriving for work, and dropping the drum into the shed."

Dockerty dug into his pocket, came out with his mobile phone and punched in the numbers.

"Detective Superintendent Dockerty is making a telephone call," Barrett reported to the recorder.

His boss spoke urgently into the phone. "It's Dockerty. Get someone down to new Britannia Parade. I want CCTV recordings for the last twenty-four hours… Yes, yes. All of it."

He cut the connection, put the phone on the table alongside his folder, and concentrated again on Joe.

"Okay, Mr Murray, let's move on again. Amongst the evidence collected at Developer's Dream, there were two items we're interested in. Ike?"

Barrett leaned down to pick up a sealed evidence bag, which he passed to Dockerty.

"I am now showing Mr Murray evidence exhibit labelled, GV-stroke-RD-stroke-one-five-stroke-one." Dockerty passed the bag to Joe and continued talking. "This is a chef's knife with an eight-inch blade and a wooden handle. The blade is badly scorched and so is the handle, but the initials L.M. can clearly be seen having been scratched into the handle. Mr Murray, do you recognise this knife?"

Holding the bag, Joe had recognised it immediately. "Yes. It belongs to my nephew, Lee."

"Lee Murray?"

"Correct." Joe took a deep breath to calm a mind already racing with ideas. "His father lives in Australia, and Lee's mother brought him back to England while he was still a boy. I became a sort of father figure to him. When he left school, he wanted to play professional rugby, but I insisted on him having a trade in case it didn't pan out. I took him on as an apprentice in the café, and sent him to catering college. It turned out to be a wise move because he suffered a knee injury playing rugby which ended his career before it got properly going. Anyway, while he was at college, I bought him a full set of chef's knives. There was a lot of thieving at that place, so Lee scratched his initials into the handles. This—" Joe held up the bag, "—is one of that set."

"I see." Dockerty considered his next words. "That knife was found on the floor of Developer's Dream, quite near to Mr Vaughan's body, and we suspect, although it make take some confirming, that it was used to stab him before the fire was started. I have to ask, Mr Murray, when did you last use that knife?"

"I don't know," Joe replied, "but I can tell you it was over a year ago."

"Why so certain?" Barrett asked.

"Because it went up in smoke with the old café."

Having delivered his coup de grace, Joe waited for a response, but he did not get one. Both police officers stared owlishly at him, waiting for more.

With an irritated cluck, he went on. "The old place was left in ruins, and according to Brad Kilburn, who was the Watch Manager that night, too, it was unsafe. I lost almost everything that night. We'd been to Blackpool for the weekend, and all I had left were the clothes I stood up in and the few in my suitcase."

"Your nephew could have taken the knives home?" Barrett asked.

"What planet are you living on, Sergeant?" Joe demanded. "Lee has a young son. You don't take lethally sharpened chef's knives home with you where an inquisitive kid might get hold of them. On the night of the fire, they were hanging on the wall in the old Lazy Luncheonette, where they always hung, and neither I, nor Lee have seen them since. I claimed a new set on the insurance."

"You don't know how that knife ended up at Vaughan's home, then?" Dockerty asked.

Joe shrugged. "I can offer you a theory, but you already know what that will be."

Dockerty mirrored the shrug and nodded to his sergeant, who produced the second piece of evidence.

The bag was labelled GV/RD/15/2 and contained a charred, Sheaffer ballpoint pen. The matte silver finish had been burned off, and Joe had no doubts that the thing was unusable, but as he turned the bag over, he once more recognised it right away.

"The pen is badly scorched, the body clearly melted in places, but the barrel of the pen is engraved on one side," Dockerty was saying to the machine. "The words are difficult to make out, but they read, 'To Joe, with thanks, Alec and Julia'." The superintendent looked up from his report. "Do you recognise that pen, Mr Murray?"

"Yes. It's mine."

"The inscription would indicate that it was a gift."

Joe nodded. "From Alec and Julia Staines. Their son, Wesley, got married last summer, or the one before. It was up in Windermere, and there was some trouble which I helped sort out with the local police."

"A drug dealer murdered," Dockerty said, checking his notes once more.

"Ten out of ten for doing your homework. Alec and Julia gave me the pen as a thank you for helping young Wes."

Barrett made a note of it. "When did you last use the pen, Mr Murray?"

"I can't say that I've ever used it. I'm not one for frills and fripperies. When I got home from Windermere, I chucked it in a drawer in my apartment."

"Your present apartment?" Dockerty wanted to know.

"No. My living quarters above the old Lazy Luncheonette. Like the knife, as far as I'm concerned, it went up with the old building. I've never seen it since, and this time I didn't claim for it on the insurance. In fact, until you just showed it to me, I'd forgotten it even existed."

"So once again, you have no idea how it came to be at Gerard Vaughan's house?"

"I have ideas, yes, but I don't *know* anything for a fact." Once again Joe sat forward. "Let's face it, all you have is someone who saw a car similar to mine, half an hour before the Fire Brigade were called, a knife which may or may not have killed Vaughan, and a pen which I haven't seen since it was first given to me. I don't know who's doing what, here, but whoever he is, he's leading you by the nose and pointing the finger at me, but you're gonna have to come up with something a lot more persuasive than this little lot."

Dockerty, too, leaned forward, resting his forearms on the table. "On the other hand, you may just have done it and be playing these tricks to double bluff us."

"Why?"

The superintendent frowned. "So we won't charge you."

"No, no, you don't understand. I don't mean why would I lay a trail like this. I mean why would I murder Vaughan in the first place?"

"You have a lot of antipathy for him," Barrett pointed out. "You admitted as much yourself."

"Yes. It's true to say I didn't like him. But I came out on top in the end."

Once more their faces were blank, and Joe let out along sigh.

"Look, Vaughan bribed his way through various council departments to get the original Britannia Parade knocked down and the new building put up."

"Unfounded allegations, Mr Murray," Barrett put in.

"True, but it's not like I'm repeating them to the press, is it?" Joe paused a moment. "Anyway, mine was the last business still operating because I wouldn't give way, and the reason I wouldn't is because Vaughan never wanted The Lazy Luncheonette in the new block. Eventually, Sanford Borough Council took out a compulsory purchase order, but I threatened to appeal it and hold them up some more. We then went away to Blackpool for the Easter weekend, and when we came back, the place had been razed to the ground."

"An act you blamed Vaughan for… er, inciting the fire, that is," Barrett said.

"I did. I had no proof, and I had no choice but to accept that he would get away with it. Anyway, they shifted me into a new building on the other side of Doncaster Road. I lost a huge amount of trade thanks to them. Then my fairy godfather turned up."

"Who?" Dockerty demanded.

"Sir Douglas Ballantyne. Don't tell me you've never heard of him. He's one of the richest men in the country. I'd sorted out some trouble at his Blackpool depot, and he was being threatened by a family member. He asked me to look into it. I did, and I pinned the perpetrator down. Sir Douglas was so grateful that he bought a majority shareholding in Gleason Holdings, Vaughan's company. He also ordered

35

Vaughan to install The Lazy Luncheonette in the new building, and at an advantageous rent for the first two years." Joe grinned. "I won."

"But Vaughan continued to make life difficult for you, didn't he?" the superintendent asked.

"He nit-picked a lot, sure. The cheeky sod even charged me rent on the cubbyhole outside where we have to store our recyclables. But his niggling was no worse than Environmental Health or even the Fire Service. I could handle it. Trust me, he was more irritated than me by the way things turned out. I even found new customers from the offices on the floors above us."

With a resigned sigh, Dockerty asked, "Is all this relevant?"

"It goes right to the heart of the matter, I'd say," Joe asserted. "What possible motive did I have for murdering him?"

"You hated him," Barrett pointed out for the second time.

"I disliked him," Joe argued. "To hate someone, you have to feel something for them, and I had no interest in him. Besides, there are plenty of people in this town who I don't like. If I had to go round killing them all, Sanford would be a ghost town. I had no motive for murdering Gerard Vaughan."

"Leaving that aside for the moment, try looking at it from our point of view, Joe. We have a murdered man, his house is burned down, and the *prima facie* evidence points at you."

"Exactly as it's meant to," Joe argued. "You know me, Dockerty. I may not be the sharpest blade under the cutlers' grindstone, but I'm not dumb. If I was gonna get rid of Vaughan, I wouldn't leave a trail leading you right back to me, would I?"

"You could have recovered the knife and pen from the old building. You could have dropped the knife after killing Vaughan, knowing that the fire would erase all forensic evidence. The pen could have fallen out of your pocket, and you couldn't know that your car was seen there."

Joe shook his head sadly. "I never went into the old building. Check Brad Kilburn's report on it. He declared it unsafe. The only people who went anywhere near it were the demolition contractors. And even if I had, why would I take a knife which could never be used again and a pen that would never work again?"

"Souvenirs," Barrett suggested.

"I'm not that sentimental," Joe retorted. "Hell's bells, I never even used the pen even though it was a gift. I repeat, you have nothing. Not even a motive. A lot of circumstantial evidence, exactly the same as Vickers had when he tried to pin the Sanford stranglings on me. Now if you can't come up with anything more concrete, can I go back to my business?"

"Not yet. I'm not entirely happy—"

Joe cut Dockerty off. "What will it take to convince you that I'm innocent?"

Quiet descended on the room. Even Joe struggled to come up with an angle that would sway the debate one way or the other.

Barrett cut into the silence. "You don't keep a mileage account for your car?"

Joe was perplexed. "Why would I?"

"Well, I was just thinking, sir, you could itemise the mileage done for business separate from your private mileage. You know, I have to log my mileage when I'm on police business so that I can claim my expenses. I thought you might do the same for tax purposes."

"My bookkeeping is complicated enough," Joe replied. "I just log the car's petrol receipts, and claim twenty percent for business. The tax and VAT people have never argued about it."

More silence, which Dockerty broke this time.

"Can you account for your movements yesterday?"

"All day?" Joe waited for the detective's agreement. "Let's see, I opened up as usual at six, and spent the day in the café. We closed at half past three, the cleaning was done by four. Sheila and Brenda went home, but I stayed behind, like I always do, checking my perishables, frozen foods and confectionery. I was short in some areas, so I made a list and then went to the very same cash and carry you mentioned, where I bought soft drinks, cakes, buns, and some frozen items: chips, ice cream, that kind of thing. I came back to the café about six-ish, put all the stuff away, then went to the Miner's Arms, where I had a couple of drinks and a snack before going home. Once home, I never went out again. I had a meal at about eight thirty, cashed up and did my books in front of the TV and then went to bed about ten fifteen. Can't be sure of the exact time, but the BBC news was on when I switched the telly off."

"What were you watching on TV?"

Joe grinned slyly. "An old episode of *Inspector Morse*. The one where his house catches fire."

"Joe." There was a warning edge to Dockerty's voice.

"Well, get your sergeant to stop asking idiot questions. I wasn't watching TV. It was just on."

Dockerty sucked in is breath. "You had no contact with Gerard Vaughan yesterday?"

"He called into the café mid-morning, moaning about the lorries parked out back."

"Delivery trucks, sir?" Barrett asked.

"No… well, yes and no. He was always moaning about the lorries delivering to us, but he was more concerned with the draymen from Sanford Brewery, and the way they crowd the lane early doors. My argument is they're usually out of the way before the office wallahs turn up, and he never moaned about trucks delivering stationery for the architects on the third floor, or the computer supplies people at street level. You know, he even blamed me for the truckers who park in the back lane overnight, and most of those are gone by the time we open."

"That was the only contact you had with him yesterday?"

Joe realised that Dockerty was fishing for something, but he was not sure what. "Unless you have evidence to the contrary, yes."

"No, I have no evidence to contradict you."

Not fishing then, other than hoping Joe might slip up and incriminate himself. "We're all over the place here, Dockerty. Do you have anything which will definitely put me in the frame for this?"

"Nothing substantial, sir, no. But think of it from my point of view. Someone went along to Vaughan's house last night and after murdering him, spread cooking oil everywhere—"

"Cooking oil." It was a eureka moment for Joe.

The detectives exchanged glances and then concentrated on Joe. "What about it?" Barrett asked.

"Listen to me for a minute, please. I know that stuff. Now let's imagine I did it. I went to his house, murdered him, then set the fire. This means taking a twenty-litre drum of cooking oil and spreading it everywhere. Once the drum was empty, there would be a film of oil all over it. You can't avoid it. If I put that in the boot of my car, there would be traces. Your forensic people will find them. I *never* carry cooking oil in my car. All right, not never, but only in extreme circumstances like when we've run out and the delivery hasn't arrived. But those are brand new drums, still sealed and they don't leave traces. Get your people to go over the boot of my car, I guarantee they will find nothing." He sat back, triumphant. "Would that persuade you that it's nothing to do with me?"

"It would help, certainly," Dockerty agreed.

"You could have cleaned the car up," Barrett argued.

"Do you have any idea how hard it is to eradicate *all* traces of oils?" Joe demanded. "It would take weeks, not minutes. If I had an empty drum of oil in my car, there will be traces and your scientific support people will find them."

"Unless you put down plastic sheeting," Barrett pointed out.

"You really are looking to hit me with this, aren't you?"

In order to stop the argument, Dockerty came to a decision. "All right, Joe, I take your point even if Sergeant Barrett doesn't. Where is your car? At the café?"

Joe nodded.

"I'll send the forensic people down there as soon as I can." The superintendent closed his folder and checked his watch. "Interview concluded at nine fifty-four."

Barrett switched off the recorder and ejected the tapes. He took out a bag and dropped one tape in it. "I'm sealing this in your presence, Mr Murray," he said, and scrawled his signature across the envelope seal. He pushed it across the desk to Joe, and handed over his pen. "If you could sign too, across the seal, please."

Joe scribbled his signature and handed it back.

Dockerty gathered together his belongings. "You're free to go for the time being, Joe, but before you do, I want to stress a couple of things. First off, you're not out of the woods. I'm letting you go because I have no further evidence to let me keep you here, but I will be looking for it. Until I say otherwise, you are still a suspect. You understand?"

"Perfectly."

"Second, I know you. You're a hard-nosed, cantankerous and stubborn old sod with an eye for detail, and no matter how much I tell you to mind your own business, you won't."

"Damn right, I won't. Not while I'm accused."

"Suspected," Dockerty corrected. "Not accused, suspected. What I'm getting at here, Joe, is you must not talk to your niece, Gemma, about this." Dockerty held his hands apart in a gesture which accepted the inevitable. "She's family and I can't stop you seeing her, but if you badger her about the case, our progress, or potential evidence, you may be trying to clear your name, but you will also be jeopardising her career. I know you're annoyed with her for the way she arrested you this morning, but she was doing her job, and according to both her and Constable Gillespie you made it impossible for her to do anything else. That aside, I'm sure you don't want to wreck her career because of your temper. If you learn anything, anything at all, which may be germane to this investigation, you must bring it to me. Once again, are we clear on this matter?"

"Yes."

Dockerty stood up. "In that case, you can go and we'll catch up with you at the café later this morning or early this afternoon."

Chapter Four

In the rear seat of the taxi taking him back to The Lazy Luncheonette, Joe struggled with a febrile mind incapable of settling on a single item from the plethora of information which had bombarded him during the morning.

Not for the first time, someone was trying to set him up for a murder he had not committed, but the major question was, why.

The last time it happened, the case of the Sanford Valentine Strangler, it was because he had had a one-night stand with the latest victim: he knew her. Was the same true this time? He knew Vaughan, he had an antagonistic business relationship with the man. Was the killer making an effort to hide his identity by capitalising on that? Or was it truly personal: someone with a grudge against Joe who had decided to deal with it in this drastic manner?

While the taxi skipped along the dual carriageway of Doncaster Road, and the tall, angular, redbrick new building came into view, Joe decided that of the two options, the latter was the more worrying. The obvious line of attack in that case would be to eventually corner and possibly kill Joe… or at the very least, see him go to prison for the rest of his life.

When it came to the matter of Vaughan's death, Joe found himself a compound of ambivalent emotions. He told himself he did not care, but at a much deeper level, the thought of ending a human life so violently and callously, filled him with anger. It was wrong. As Dockerty had pointed out, it was a crime and the perpetrator needed to be locked away.

"If I had my way, I'd hang them," he said to Sheila and

Brenda after relating the morning's events to them.

Sheila tutted. "And then send apologies to all those innocent men you've executed?"

"No, Sheila. With DNA—"

"Joe, no one has the right to take another human being's life," Sheila argued. "Not even the state. Lock them up forever, if you have to, but if life is God-given, then only God can take it away."

Joe shut up. Sheila was not particularly evangelical, but her faith was one of the bedrocks of her life, and such arguments were a sure way to major rows.

Brenda tactfully changed the subject. "So, are we in the same boat as we were when they accused you of being the Valentine Strangler?"

"Not quite," Joe replied. "Dockerty might be a hard nut, but he's fair, and he doesn't have the downer on me that Vickers had. I'm not likely to find my name plastered all over the *Sanford Gazette* this afternoon." He slurped on a beaker of tea. "If it's gonna be a long, drawn out affair, we'll have to call Les Tanner and ask him to stand as chairman of the 3rd Age Club until I get it sorted. But once they check my car over, they'll know it's nothing to do with me and we should be back to normal."

The Lazy Luncheonette experienced a mid-morning lull every day from nine fifteen, by which time the brewery drivers were gone, and eleven o'clock when the first shoppers from Sanford Retail Park, seeking more wholesome and often cheaper fare than offered by the fast food outlets in the mall, began to arrive.

Since moving into the new premises, with all those offices above them, there had been a slight increase in morning trade as the staff came down for takeaway orders, but even that was over by nine thirty.

A hot Tuesday in July was no exception and while Joe enjoyed a beaker of tea at table five, in front of the counter (so numbered because the same table had always been his favourite in the old café) the rest of the room was empty. In the open plan kitchen, Lee was busy preparing lunches, and

43

his wife Cheryl, was helping. Sheila and Brenda sat with Joe, Sheila concentrating on a magazine and Brenda writing a letter, leaving him the kind of quiet he wanted when coming to grips with a puzzle of this nature.

Taking out a notebook, he began to write a list, but it had nothing to do with shopping.

Brenda glanced sideways from her letter and asked, "What are you weighing up, Joe?" She leaned closer and read aloud. "Firemen, cops, passers-by, scroats… demolishers?" Brenda laughed. "Is there such a word?"

"I don't know," Joe replied. "I'm trying to work out who could have got a hold of that pen and knife."

"Well, I'd cross out passers-by," Sheila commented looking up from her magazine. "After the fire was put out, the site was fenced off."

Brenda giggled. "And I'd change demolishers to demolition crew, because I'm still not sure demolishers is a proper word."

"Go back to writing… who are you writing to, anyway?"

"My cousin, June. You remember her. She met a Canadian while she was in the army, and settled down over there."

Joe nodded and then spoke to Sheila. "Someone passing by could have climbed over the fence."

"Then they'd be scroats, not passers-by," Sheila retorted. "Anyway, the person who did this is, by definition, a scroat. It was deliberate, Joe. You'd be better off scrubbing both scroats and passers-by, and concentrating on the people who don't like you."

Abandoning her letter for the second time, Brenda laughed again. "He doesn't have enough pages in the notebook for them."

Joe dismissed her opinion with a grunt and went back to his list.

A thought occurred to Sheila. "You know, whoever did this was planning for the long term, wasn't he?"

The other two looked up from their lists. "You're assuming it's a man," Joe said.

"How do you mean, Sheila?" Brenda asked, more pertinently.

"The old place burned down over a year ago. They must have picked up the pen and the knife on the night-stroke-day of the fire. They've hung onto them for fifteen months. That begs the question, were they planning on murdering Vaughan all along, and if so, why wait until now?" She put down her magazine. "Think about your situation, Joe. You've all but beaten Vaughan, albeit thanks to Sir Douglas Ballantyne. There were niggles, I'll grant you, but they were no worse than you get from some other people. If you were going to murder Vaughan, surely it would have been while we were across the road in that awful, temporary place. Not now."

Joe scowled. "I already told the cops all of that."

***

The post-lunch lull had set in by the time Detective Sergeant Barrett and the forensic officers turned up at half past one, and Joe was up to his elbows in helping wash those items which would not fit in the dishwasher; large pans, strainers, grill trays and such.

In contrast to his hostility earlier in the day, Barrett was friendly enough, but business-like and obviously keen to get on with the job. "We've been ordered to go over your car, sir, and check the skips for any signs of discarded plastic sheeting."

"You'll find the spare key for the car on a hook over there," Joe said, gesturing to a rack where coats and other items of kitchen clothing hung. "I'll let you get on with it. We have enough to do."

Barrett nodded at the three-man forensic team. "I have to speak to building security," he announced.

"I thought Dockerty had already secured the tapes."

"We tried," Barrett agreed with a nod, "but when our man got here, they weren't ready. They're no longer using videotape. They're digital and we need to take copies of the files." He held up a couple of memory sticks.

"Whaddya mean 'no longer using videotape'?" Joe demanded. "No one's used tape for years."

"Which is exactly what I meant, sir."

Barrett left, and Malcolm Devere, the head of the forensic team, his face mostly covered by a mask, was left to study the tiled wall in the corner where Joe had indicated.

At length he asked, "Excuse me, Mr Murray, but you did say the car key was here?"

"There. On the hook…." Joe trailed off looking where the forensic man stood, and a small, shallow, stick-on hook, where a bunch of general keys hung. There was no sign of the car key. He called out into the dining area. "Who took the sandwiches this morning?"

"I did," Sheila replied.

"You've still got the spare car key in your pocket."

"I don't think so," Sheila said, rooting into the large pocket of her tabard. Her cheeks coloured as she came out with the keys. "Sorry, Joe."

He tutted and said to the forensic officer, "It's always happening." Drying a pan from the bain-marie, he nodded at the waste bin beneath the hooks. "Either that or the keys fall off into the bin."

"We lost 'em altogether the other week," Lee commented. "Fell in the bin, no one noticed and we chucked 'em out."

"Yeah," Joe said, passing the pan back to Lee. "And it cost me nearly eighty quid for a new one."

The forensic man took the key from Sheila and looked at the red tab on the back corner of the plastic surround. "Chipped, is it?"

"No alarm fitted," Joe confirmed. "but the key disables the immobiliser."

"Right, Mr Murray. I'll get out and get on with. Through the back?" He pointed at the rear open door.

Joe nodded again. "Black Ford Ka. It's the only one there and it should be parked near the door."

Half an hour passed. With most of the cleaning done, and

few callers (Joe guessed people preferred to be out in the sunshine rather than sitting in a café facing away from the sun) Lee and Cheryl went home, and Joe, Sheila and Brenda seated themselves at table five, Joe ruminating on the crossword in the Daily Express, Sheila reading her magazine, Brenda picking up her letter again. Barrett came through and disappeared via the back door to join the forensic team.

A further half hour went by with only one customer dropping in, and Joe was about to call it a day when Barrett came back in through the rear door.

"I'm sorry, Mr Murray, but could you come out here, please?"

"Problems?" Joe asked, getting to his feet and draining off his tea.

"If you could just come with me, sir."

Sheila and Brenda exchanged concerned glances as Joe and Barrett passed through the kitchen and out into the back lane.

Gleason Holdings had purchased a large chunk of land behind the old Britannia Parade, and levelled and tarmacked it to provide a parking area for the office workers. Joe was always first to arrive every morning and parked his car close to the rear door of The Lazy Luncheonette, but across the expanse of tarmac, the car park was now almost full.

Standing at the open boot of the Ford Ka, two forensic officers, both wearing white jumps suits, had abandoned their face masks and were smoking cigarettes. The third, Devere, was in the driver's seat of his van, making notes.

With Barrett's approach, the two men stubbed out their cigarettes and moved to one side.

Before guiding Joe to the boot of the car, Barrett spoke in tones that were anything but reassuring. "Now, Mr Murray, during the interview this morning, you did say that you never carry empty cans of cooking oil in your car."

"Never."

"Malc?"

Devere climbed out of the van, bringing his clipboard

47

with him, and led them to the rear of Joe's car.

The boot was empty, save for a bag of wheel-changing tools. Its grey carpet appeared spotlessly clean to Joe, but small areas had been circled in blue dye by the forensic team.

"We've photographed everything for reference." Devere consulted his clipboard. "We found traces of cooking oil in several places. There is also an area—" He pointed to a larger, more elliptical marking on the carpet, "—where a drum has stood. From the arc of cooking oil left on the carpet, we can calculate the diameter of the receptacle, and we estimate that it must have been a standard, twenty-litre drum."

The colour drained from Joe's tanned features.

Barrett was no more and no less pleasant yet business-like than he had been all morning. "How do you explain that, Mr Murray?"

"I, er... I don't. I can't."

"From what Malcolm tells me, Mrs Riley had the keys, and took the vehicle out this morning. Could she have placed a drum of oil in the boot?"

"What? No, of course not." Joe was not about to let the police even try to lay the blame on one of his employees. "She takes sandwiches to Ingleton Engineering. It's a small firm about a mile down the road." He waved in the general direction of Sanford town centre. "It's not a big order. They're bagged up individually and she carries them in a cardboard box. She wouldn't even open the boot."

"This engineering company wouldn't have need of a drum of cooking oil?"

"We've been supplying them with sandwiches for forty years, and they've never asked for one yet."

"You see the position we're in, sir," Barrett explained. "During your interview this morning, you assured us that your car had not moved since you got home last night. You also assured us, and you've just repeated that you never carry drums of cooking oil, other than new and unused, in the boot of this car. So I have to ask, how come the cooking oil got there? How come there was a drum, which appears to have been opened at some point, allowing the traces of oil to spill, in your car boot?"

"And I've already said, I don't know. Other than me or one of the girls when they took out the sandwich order, no one has been near that car since… I can't remember when." He turned on Devere. "You're sure it is cooking oil?"

"No doubt about it," the forensic officer replied.

"The same oil I use?"

Devere shrugged, "I'd have to have a sample of your oil to compare. Can you give me one?"

"I'll get a drum from the kitchen."

Joe took a pace forward before Devere stopped him.

"It would be better if we could take a sample from an old drum, Joe. Fresh oil would not be contaminated and it may lead us to the wrong conclusion."

"You mean it may prove me innocent?"

Devere remained ambivalent under Joe's sour eye. "Or guilty."

Joe pointed at the back wall alongside The Lazy Luncheonette's rear exit, where a single, metal door, in pale turquoise stood locked. The upper half bore louvre slats for ventilation, and although it was strong in appearance, it was double secured with a brass padlock, and an inset mortise lock.

"Keys?" Devere asked.

"In the kitchen on the same hook as the car keys… should have been."

"Double locked?" Barrett asked while they waited for the forensic man to reappear.

"We had a lot of trouble in the old place," Joe explained. "There was a back yard there, and we had a shed at the bottom where we stored the old drums and other material for recycling. Cardboard and the like. Kids used to break in regular, nicking the drums and stuff, so I set up two padlocks. Course, they went up in smoke with the building, but when we moved into this place, I took one look at the cheap lock on that cupboard door and thought, no way.

They'll jemmy it in minutes. So I bought a brass padlock for it."

"Not worth that much, are they?" Barrett asked. "The drums, I mean?"

"I get two or three pounds each off the recycling man. It's not that, though. It's the mess the thieving gits create when they break into cupboards like this. You should know. You must see plenty of it."

Devere returned and after collecting sealed sample tubes and a funnel from his van, tried to unlock the door. Joe and Barrett watched with interest as he tried to turn the key. At length, he checked the other keys on the ring, trying one or two.

Joe took them from him. "Here. Give me the damn things. I dunno. Bloody cops. Can't even open a padlock with the…"

He trailed off as he, too, found it impossible to turn the key in the padlock. With a frown of puzzlement, he ran through the keys on the ring until he found the one he was seeking, and inserted it into the door lock. He turned it and the door opened, but only a fraction of an inch before the padlock stopped it. Trying the padlock key once more, he found he could not open it.

"Strange. Probably seized up, eh? I have some three-in-one oil in the café. That should loosen it." He handed the keys back to Devere and hurried into the kitchen, where he spent a few moments going through his general store cupboard, where, amongst the washing up pads, detergents and other general, non-food necessities, he dug out a small can of oil.

Rushing back out, he tilted the lock upwards and with the can's plastic feed pressed to the padlock keyhole, squeezed a few drops in.

"It'll take a minute," he promised as he returned to the kitchen and put the can of oil away.

When he got back outside, it was to find Devere trying the lock and shrugging his shoulders.

"Joe, this is the wrong key."

"It's the right key," Joe insisted. "It's just needs a bit more time for the oil to soak through."

With another shrug, Devere backed off to wait.

"Have you had trouble with this lock before, sir?" Barrett asked.

"Never," Joe assured him. "We're in this cupboard every day. Chucking in cardboard, waste paper, plastics, and, obviously, the used cooking oil drums. It was probably a bit nippy last night and the lock is iced up."

Even to himself the excuse sounded hollow. The temperature had not dropped much below 15 degrees overnight.

Devere said so. "Joe, it's been hot enough to fry eggs on the patio overnight."

"Then maybe there's some muck got in the lock."

"It's the wrong key," the forensic man insisted, and stepped forward to try it one more time.

"And I'm telling you it's the right key," Joe said, his temper beginning to get the better of him.

Devere came away again, unable to open the padlock. "Sergeant Barrett, this is the wrong key for this padlock."

Barrett faced Joe, his features now grim. "Mr Murray, it looks to me like you may have something to hide in there."

"Don't talk so bloody stupid, man."

"I'm sorry, but given this problem, and the traces of oil we found in your car, I'm going to have to take you back to the station for further questioning. I'm also going to insist that the café is closed and remains closed so our forensic officers can work on it, and I'll need all the keys to your flat."

"No way are you searching my flat. Listen, Barrett—"

"We'll obtain a warrant to search it, sir. My main concern in asking for the keys is that none of your friends can go there and disturb any potential evidence."

"How dare you?" Sheila said, making all of them aware that she and Brenda had appeared at the back door.

""Madam?" Barrett asked.

"How dare you insinuate that Brenda or I would go to

51

Joe's flat without his permission, and how dare you imply that we might tamper with evidence? My husband was a respected police officer in this town, and both Brenda and I are law-abiding citizens." She glowered at the young detective. "So is Joe."

"I'm sure he is, Mrs Riley." Nonplussed by her anger, Barrett recovered quickly. Taking his mobile phone, he punched in a number. "This is Detective Sergeant Barrett. I'm at the rear of The Lazy Luncheonette, on Doncaster Road. I'm sealing the place off until forensics can go through it. Right now, I want an officer to go to Flat 21, Queen's Court, Leeds Road Estate and tape off the front door as a possible crime or evidence scene... Yes, now... I don't care how shorthanded you are, get it done, and if you want to argue about it, speak to Detective Superintendent Dockerty."

He cut the connection and dropped the phone in his pocket before giving orders to Devere. "Tape the place off, Malcolm. When your boys can get on it, search the place for other keys, if you can't find one, check with Ray Dockerty and snap that padlock off. I want to know what's in that cupboard. While you're at it, get onto the wrecker." He threw out an arm indicating Joe's Ford. "I want this car towed to the forensic garage, and you go through it with the proverbial."

While Devere and his small team gathered themselves to carry out his orders, digging out the scene-of-crime tape and fully suiting up again, Barrett took out his handcuffs and rounded on Joe.

"You, Mr Murray, are coming with me, and if you resist, I will cuff you."

Chapter Five

There were few niceties this time. Once booked into the station, Joe was shown, not to the interview rooms, but a cell, to wait for the senior investigators.

And it would be a long wait. Locked into the cell just after four in the afternoon, it was after seven when he was finally escorted to the interview room where Dockerty and Barrett were waiting for him.

He had passed the time racking his brains for an explanation covering the things the police had found, and he had come to only one conclusion.

"This entire business is a fit up," he declared on entering the interview room.

Dockerty said nothing, but indicated to Barrett that he should set up the recorder. The sergeant spent a few minutes opening fresh cassette tapes (and demonstrating to Joe that they were brand new) labelling them and inserting them into the machine. Once it was running they identified themselves, and Dockerty advised Joe.

"When we questioned you this morning, you declined to call your solicitor. I'm advising you now, Mr Murray, in the light of fresh evidence, that you should call your lawyer."

"I'll play it by ear," Joe said. "Come on too strong, and I'll bring him in."

"As you wish," Dockerty said, giving Joe the impression that he disapproved.

The senior detective opened up his folder and spread papers out in front of him. Joe could not see what remained in the folder, but two pieces looked like photographs.

"Mr Murray," Dockerty began. "Earlier today Detective Sergeant Barrett, along with a small team of forensic officers, visited Britannia Parade and your premises in that building. They collected digital video recordings taken from CCTV cameras posted front and rear of the building. They also collected samples from the boot of your car, which indicated the presence of cooking oil, despite your earlier assurance to us that you never, repeat never carry used drums in your car. The forensic team also established that a container for oil, a cylindrical drum, had been in the boot. Their calculations, based on the arc of the trace oil, indicate a twenty-litre drum, similar to the ones you use in the course of your business. You were unable to satisfactorily account for any of this. Are you able to account for it now?"

"It was planted there," Joe said. "It's the only explanation."

Barrett stepped in. "Just so we can be clear on this, sir, the forensic team were alone when they examined the car boot, and I was not with you, either. I was elsewhere in the building. Are you insinuating that either I or the forensic officers planted the drum and the oil in your car?"

Joe shook his head. "No. I'm offering an explanation, not making an accusation. You and your people obviously had the opportunity to set this up, but it would be a stroke of luck beyond belief if you managed to get the right oil in the right drum, and unless one of you killed Vaughan and you're trying to pin it on me, I don't see what you would gain."

"However, you insist someone is trying to set this up to make you appear guilty?" Dockerty asked.

"Like I said, it's the only explanation."

"Very well," Dockerty said, and studied his reports for a moment. "Forensic Practitioner, Malcolm Devere asked you for a sample of old cooking oil, yet when you attempted to open the door to your recycling shed, you could not. You said the lock was jammed or seized. Our people, on my authorisation, used bolt cutters to remove the padlock, which was taken back to the forensic laboratory in Leeds for further examination. The result of that examination indicates that the key did not fit that lock." He looked up and held Joe's gaze. "How do you react to that?"

"Someone changed the lock," Joe replied.

"It's interesting that you should say that, because—"

Dockerty was about to dig into his folder again, but Joe interrupted.

"Coming back to the cooking oil, has it been analysed?"

The senior man tutted and searched through his documents again. When he found the right one, he read through it, and announced. "Preliminary analysis indicates that it is the same brand as the one you use."

"Is it from the same batch?"

The two detectives exchanged glances.

"Again, Mr Murray?" Barrett asked.

Now Joe tutted. "What I know about cooking oil production, you could write on a postcard, and still leave room for greetings to your mum. But it's produced in batches of god knows how many thousands of litres at a time. I take a delivery of one hundred litres per month … on average. Now, I ask again, does the oil they found in my car match up with the batches I have in stock, or the traces left in the empty drums? Because if it doesn't, you're gonna have trouble proving I ever owned it, never mind put it in the boot."

"That will be a matter for the prosecution and defence counsels should we go to trial," Dockerty declared. He leaned forward. "Listen to me, Joe. I'd like to believe you're innocent. I don't see you as the kind of man who could perpetrate this sort of crime. But there is too much here that you can't explain, and lacking evidence to point us in any other direction, you are in serious trouble."

"I did explain," Joe argued. "Someone is setting me up. I've just asked you if the oil is from the same batch I use, and I told you someone must have changed the lock on the storage shed."

"Ah." Dockerty sounded triumphant. "I'm glad you brought us back to that… again. Now, before I move on, can you confirm your earlier statement that your car never left your home during the night?"

"I parked up between half past seven and eight o'clock last night, it didn't move again until gone five this morning."

"Then perhaps you can explain these images."

Dockerty spread three large monochrome photographs on the table and turned them to face Joe.

"These are still images taken from the CCTV at the rear of Britannia Parade. Note the time stamp." He pointed to the lower section of the image where the camera ID was printed in bold white, and alongside it, the time stamp. "In this first image, Mr Murray, we can see a Ford Ka. We can't ascertain the colour, because the image is monochrome, but it's obviously a dark shade. We can, however, clearly see the rear number-plate, and it bears your registration."

Joe studied the image. It was, indeed, his registration, and it did look like his car.

"If I was going to frame me, the first thing I would do is find an old car like mine and set it up with false plates."

"You insist, then, that this is not your car?"

"I told you. My car never moved."

"And I don't believe you, Mr Murray, because there are too many factors which say exactly the opposite. Look at the next two images." Dockerty removed the image of the car and moved the remaining two into the middle of the table.

The first showed a car stopped at the rear of The Lazy Luncheonette. It was some distance from the camera, and the image was grainy, but it clearly showed a dark-clothed man climbing out of the car in close proximity to Joe's storage shed. In the second image, the man was brandishing a pair of heavy duty bolt cutters. The angle was very shallow, but he appeared to be working on the shed's padlock.

"The original CCTV footage shows him cut the lock off, then place a drum in the shed. He then puts on a fresh lock."

"A proper fit up," Joe murmured. He looked up at the two detectives. "It isn't me."

"He's too far from the camera, and the image is too hazy

to see who he is, sir," Barrett pointed out. "And frankly, I believe it is you."

"I don't care what you believe. I'm telling you, it isn't me."

Dockerty intervened before a major argument could break out. "Joe, look at this logically. You say your car never moved and it never carried cooking oil. Yet we have evidence that it did move. There are soil samples in the driver's footwell which can only have come from Eastward. We have it on CCTV in Back Britannia Parade after the fire at Vaughan's house was started, and we have traces of cooking oil in the boot."

"Yes but—"

"Our forensic boys are going over that car as we speak," Dockerty cut in. "There will be other traces and they will find them. The batch test you mentioned, will be carried out on the oil, although in itself it proves nothing, and we will match it up. We have one of your nephew's knives taken from the scene of the crime, we have a pen, which you admit belongs to you, taken from the scene of the crime. I don't know what the jiggery-pokery with the padlock was all about, but it seems to me you were hoping we wouldn't need access to that shed. Well, we have access and everything in there will be thoroughly checked over. We will also go through the café and your home with a fine-toothed comb. As far as I'm concerned, Joe, although there's a long way to go, I'm satisfied that you did it." Dockerty paused to let the import of his words sink in. "Just get it all off your chest."

Across the table, Joe stared miserably at his hands. Inside he was a turmoil of absolute fury, and the frustration at being unable to unleash that anger only added to the fires.

He looked up and glared at them. "I am innocent. And right now I want my solicitor."

"Fine. Joseph Murray, I am holding you on suspicion of the murder of Gerard Vaughan. I must caution you..."

The rest of the official caution was lost on Joe as he sank into an even deeper depression.

***

Sheila received a call from Gemma at eight. An hour later, after some urgent ringing round, she and Brenda met with Gemma, Les Tanner and Sylvia Goodson in the bar of the Miner's Arms, where Gemma brought them up to date.

It was a typical Tuesday evening. The bar was almost empty, the TV played largely to itself, and the staff stood behind their counter, occasionally yawning, constantly checking the time.

As she listened, Sheila, chairing the impromptu meeting, found her anger growing.

Gemma was suitably apologetic. "I can't tell you anything about the investigation, nor the evidence we have, but I can tell you it's pretty compelling."

"Absurd is what it is," Sheila snapped. "Joe is no more a murderer than you or I."

"I called you, Mrs Riley, because Joe has few people in the way of family. Only me, and I can hardly be said to be neutral, and Lee, and let's be honest, Lee wouldn't have a clue how to help his uncle. You people are his closest friends, and the only ones who can help."

"Help in what say, Gemma?" Tanner asked. "According to what you've told us, he has his solicitor."

Gemma looked away. She downed a swift mouthful of vodka and swallowed a lump in her throat with it. When she faced them again, there was the hint of sparkling tears in the corner of her eyes.

"They were still interviewing him when I rang you, Mrs Riley, but right now, it looks as if Joe did it."

"Nonsense."

"I'm sorry, Mrs Riley, but that's how it appears."

Brenda was as hard as Sheila. "It's been made to look like that."

"So Joe says, but there is too much he cannot explain, and it all points at him. He'll appear in court tomorrow and he'll be remanded. Whether on bail or in custody, he'll be allowed access to you, which is why I came to see you. If you really want to help him, persuade him to come clean. The amount of grief he took from Vaughan will go some way to mitigating the crime. It's still murder, he's still looking at a life sentence, but if he confesses and shows some genuine remorse, the tariff will be reduced."

The silence which greeted her announcement could not have been more stunning if she had announced that Joe had murdered every one of his competitors in Yorkshire.

It was Sheila who broke it. "I find it hard to imagine that you believe all this, Gemma, and I refuse to be party to any attempts to persuade Joe he's better off pleading guilty." She jabbed her finger into the table top. "He is innocent, and the best way we, his friends, can help, is to prove that."

Gemma finished her drink and made ready to leave. "Fine. If you can do so, then we'll listen. I'm sorry. Trust me, I really am sorry. He's my uncle and he went out of his way to help me when I first signed on with the police. I don't want to see him in this position, but facts are facts. You will be allowed access, assuming he's happy to see you. Speak to Mr Dockerty in the morning. For now, I'll bid you goodnight."

They watched her march from the bar, and Tanner rose to refresh their drinks.

"You should calm down, Sheila," Sylvia said. "It's not good for your gallstones to get so het up."

"It's difficult when your employer is locked up," Brenda said. "And they've closed The Lazy Luncheonette, you know. Right now, all we can do is sit in the café while the forensic people go over it."

"This is a… oh what's the word?" Sheila groped into thin air for the correct phrase.

"Railroad? Fit up? Frame?" Brenda suggested.

"However you want to express it," she agreed as Tanner returned with fresh drinks. "Someone is making Joe appear guilty, and the police are following the line like sheep."

Settling into his seat, Tanner asked, "So what do you want to do?"

"We need to move quickly," she replied. "First, we need

to call an extraordinary meeting on the 3rd Age Club. Brenda and I will ring the core members tomorrow. They can spread the word. In Joe's absence, we'll need a chair *pro tem*, and I'd like you to take it on, Les. We can put it to the vote tomorrow night, but it will be a pure formality."

"Naturally, I will do what I can, and I'm happy to take the mantle."

Sheila grunted her acceptance and sipped her gin and tonic. "Beyond that, we need to employ some of Joe's techniques."

Brenda laughed. "Treat everyone with contempt? Snap at them?"

Her best friend scowled, and Sylvia, too, pursed her lips in disapproval.

"Come on," Brenda urged. "I'm only trying to lighten the mood."

"I hope you'll remember that, Brenda, when Joe is given a life sentence for a crime he didn't commit."

A broody silence followed Sheila's dire prognostication.

"Joe did have a grudge against this awful man," Sylvia pointed out.

"No. He didn't like Vaughan, I'll grant you. Very few people did. But Joe had won the war. He had no reason to kill Vaughan…" Sheila trailed off, noticing that Les had suddenly lapsed into deep thought, a frown creasing his normally clear brow. "Something wrong, Les?"

"Not wrong, exactly. I'm just wondering about what you said. Joe had no reason to kill Vaughan because he had won the war. Let's recap, and tell me where I may have it wrong. After the old Lazy Luncheonette burned down, you were moved to the opposite side of Doncaster Road, and trade suffered."

"Badly," Brenda confirmed. "But then Sir Douglas Ballantyne stepped in, bought out Gleason Holdings and insisted that we were given a prime spot in the new parade."

"And Vaughan was never happy with that."

"Correct." Sheila's gimlet eye lay firmly on Les. "Where are you going with this?"

"Old Ballantyne retired. Some time ago, as I understand it. He handed the reins to his son, Toby. Has Toby had a change of heart? Has he decided he's more interested in mail order than property? Did he hand everything back to Vaughan and if so, was Vaughan ready to pile the pressure on Joe again?"

"You sound as though you believe Joe is guilty," Sheila complained.

"Nothing of the kind. I'm trying to look at things objectively. Sheila, your late husband was a police officer. He would know, and so should you, that Joe would need a motive for killing Vaughan. I'm simply suggesting one."

"And that would make it all the more difficult to prove Joe's innocence," Brenda pointed out.

Sheila slapped her hand on the table causing several of the pub's sparse patrons to look in their direction. "I won't hear any more of this," Sheila said. "Joe is innocent. Let the police look for darker motives. What we need to do is look for alternative killers, and to do that, we need to employ the same skills Joe does. Observation and simple logic."

Tanner and Brenda acquiesced under Sheila's temper.

"Very well," Tanner agreed. "I can think of one or two likely candidates in the town hall. I'll have a word with them."

"Oh, Les, don't risk your livelihood," Sylvia fretted.

"Have you forgotten the time Joe cleared your name, Sylvia?" Sheila asked. "He's placed his head on the block for quite a few of us. You, George Robson, Brenda. He's put himself at risk of arrest for harassing the police in our favour. It's time we repaid some of that trust." Taking a deep breath and another sip of gin, she went on, "I will speak to Sir Douglas tomorrow morning. I'll also speak to Superintendent Dockerty. If they lock him up, I'm sure Brenda and I will be able to see Joe. One way or another, we must help him. Are we all agreed?"

No one dissented.

"Good. Time we all went home and got some sleep. It's going to be a busy few days."

Chapter Six

Notwithstanding their late finish the previous evening, Dockerty and Barrett were back in Sanford by eight the following morning and with Joe due in court at ten, Dockerty was accounting for his actions to the station commander.

"I have enough evidence to hold him."

"You can't hold him here?" Oughton asked.

Dockerty shook his head. "Either way I'll still need a magistrate to remand him, and frankly, Don, you don't have enough bodies to supervise a prisoner in this station. Let Sanford nick look after him. I know he's a friend—"

"That's irrelevant," Oughton interrupted. "Although, I have to say I'm disappointed in him." He allowed himself a moment of self-pity. "I assume that once he's remanded you'll be looking for more evidence. Something more concrete than you have."

"I've already closed down the café and I'll be asking for warrants to search there and his home. Right now I don't have one piece of evidence that relates directly to him, but indirectly, we have him banged to rights. That's why he called his lawyer."

"I just hope we're not jumping the gun, Ray."

Dockerty shrugged his huge shoulders. "Wouldn't be the first time, and if I'm wrong, then I'll apologise. But I'm not wrong. Devere in forensics assures us that the soil samples in the footwell of Joe's car can only have come from the area where Vaughan lived. Joe's car was there. Joe swears his car stayed where it was all night on Monday. It didn't, and if it was at Vaughan's, then it was also at the back of the café coming up to midnight. And if he insists he didn't loan it to anyone, which he did at the first interview, then he was the one driving it. That, plus the traces of oil in the boot, clinch it for me."

"The CCTV video doesn't identify him," Oughton pointed out.

"The CCTV doesn't identify anyone," Dockerty countered. "The camera is set on a wide-angle and it's too far from that rear shed for us to make out any features. I said, Don, we're waiting for more direct evidence. In the meantime, I have to press ahead with the remand. If I don't and it turns out he's guilty, we get hung drawn and quartered."

"If we do you'll be slaughtered anyway. Joe has a lot of enemies, so to speak, in this town, but he has a lot more friends. I've already had Sheila Riley on the phone complaining about the way he's been treated."

Dockerty tutted. "I thought your friendship didn't matter."

"It doesn't. If Joe is guilty, then we'll take it all the way. But I'm the station commander, Ray, and the man who has to deal with the, er, political and community fallout from a case like this." Oughton smiled wistfully. "I imagine it's less of a problem in a big city like Leeds."

"True, but we still have it to deal with." Dockerty checked his watch. "We're in court at ten. I'd better get a move on."

"Joe's seen his solicitor?"

"Fella called Hagley. Joe's with him now."

"Then I'll let you get to it, Ray. And keep me posted."

With a brisk nod, Dockerty left Oughton's office and made his way along to the cramped CID room, where his small team comprising Gemma, Barrett, one other detective constable and a few uniformed officers were gathered, talking amongst themselves, waiting for his arrival.

At the front of the room was a whiteboard where the evidence so far had been listed. Photographs of Joe, Vaughan's house and one of the dead man, but not an image of him as he was after the fire. It looked as if it had been taken from his company files. These photographs were mingled with others from the CCTV and those taken by the forensic officers. Various notes had been made with different coloured dry-wipe marker pens. Green constituted their suspicions, black indicated absolute facts, red highlighted lines of enquiry still open, and blue for lines of inquiry still to be instigated.

Dockerty stood front and centre, and surveyed his crew. With the exception of himself and Barrett, all were Sanford-based, and it showed in their distrustful eyes.

"Morning, everyone. This won't take long. It can't. I'm in court in an hour." He grinned. "It's all right. I'm sure I'll be let off with a caution."

The opening shaft fell flat. Aside from Barrett no one registered a hint of a smile.

Dockerty pressed on. "All right. To bring you up to speed, Joe Murray is being held on suspicion of the Gerard Vaughan's murder. He'll appear before the magistrates at ten o'clock and he'll be remanded, probably to HM Prison, Sanford."

Gemma tutted, and Dockerty homed in on her while still speaking to the rest of the room.

"Because of her family relationship to Mr Murray, Detective Inspector Craddock cannot lead this investigation, which is why I and Sergeant Barrett have come over from Leeds. It's unusual for a superintendent to get out there and ask the questions, but we're so short of bodies, I have no choice. I will be out and about, and I will conduct any and every interview at the station." He injected more force into his voice. "I know how you all feel about this. The big boots from Leeds are trampling all over one of Sanford's loveable pains in the arse who wouldn't hurt a fly. I don't care how much we're hurting your feelings, and I don't care about Joe Murray's oh-so-innocent past. We have incontrovertible evidence that his car was involved at the murder scene on Monday night, and since he insists that the car never moved from outside his home, he is obviously lying and that in turn, means he moved it. As things stand, Joe Murray is guilty, and that will be the situation until I have evidence to the contrary."

Gemma raised her hand and Dockerty raised his eyebrows at her.

"Incontrovertible evidence, sir?"

"There is no doubt that Joe's car was at the scene," Dockerty repeated, "and despite his denials, he had been carrying cooking oil in the car boot. I'll bring you up to speed properly after the court hearing, Gemma. Right now, I can tell you that we have more evidence than that, and I don't just mean the pen and knife found at the scene." The superintendent returned to addressing the room. "The evidence is pretty persuasive, otherwise I would not have charged him, but right at this moment, we have nothing to link him directly to the murder. The Lazy Luncheonette has been closed on my orders. We have the keys to Murray's apartment and that has been sealed off. Inspector Craddock will divide you into two teams. Team A will go to The Lazy Luncheonette. Inspector Craddock will contact either Mrs Jump or Mrs Riley to ensure they're there with the keys. Team B will go to Murray's flat. In both instances, you will turn the place over looking for anything, *anything at all* which may help our case—"

"What about the stuff that may hinder our case?" Vinny Gillespie called out.

Dockerty glowered at him. "Open your mouth like that again, Gillespie, and I'll suspend you."

Vinny backed down. "Sorry, sir. It didn't come out like I meant it to. I meant what about evidence that may prove him innocent."

Slightly mollified, Dockerty went back to addressing the room. "If you, any of you, can bring me evidence like that, then do so. I'm not here to crucify Joe Murray. I'm here to put a murderer behind bars, and if Joe is innocent, then I don't want to see him in prison one moment longer than is necessary." He pointed to the whiteboard and the CCTV images. "Murray's car was captured on security cameras in Back Britannia Parade at about a quarter to midnight." He moved on to the photograph of the dark figure climbing out of the car. "He was seen getting out of the car and cutting off the lock to the recycling shed. Was it Murray? Traces of cooking oil in the boot of his car, and soil samples from the driver's footwell say it was. Murray insists the car was a ringer. Team B, talk to his neighbours at Queen's Court. Did any of them see or hear his car being driven away at about ten thirty on Monday night. Team A, I want a count of all drums of cooking oil, full and empty, at The Lazy Luncheonette. Team A, I want the skips and dumpsters behind The Lazy Luncheonette checked seven ways from Sunday. I don't know if they've been collected this week, but you're looking for a padlock which has been snapped off with bolt cutters. You're also looking for an empty drum of cooking oil which may or may not be there. No one else in that building uses the stuff, so if you find one, it has to have come from either The Lazy Luncheonette or from this bloke with the car… if it turns out not to be Murray." He scanned the small group again. "Any questions?"

"Joe's netbook and smartphone, sir?" Gemma asked. "We all know he likes to keep track of his life on that computer, and his call history might push us one way or the other."

"We already have his phone," Dockerty reported. "He had it on him when he was brought in last night. The netbook, I didn't know about, so thanks, Gemma. Team B, when you're searching his flat bring back the netbook, if you can find it, and any other computer he may have there. Remember, for the moment, we're presuming Joe to be guilty, but it's just as important that you bring back anything that may prove otherwise. If Joe is innocent, I want to know, because I shall want to get on the track of the real killer. Anything else?"

No one volunteered and Dockerty dismissed them. While they began to file out, chattering amongst themselves, Barrett and Gemma approached the senior man.

"Forensic report came in while you were with Chief Superintendent Oughton, sir," Barrett said. "Vaughan's laptop, salvaged from the fire."

"What about it?"

"The hard drive had been removed."

"Removed?"

"Yes, sir," Barrett confirmed. "The back of the computer had been taken off and the hard drive removed. Not rived out or anything."

"That's it, then," Gemma declared. "It wasn't Joe."

His patience wearing thin, Dockerty asked, "Why?"

"Sir, he knows how to use computers. He's good on the internet and word processing stuff, and how to keep his accounts straight. But he hasn't a clue about hardware. He wouldn't know a hard drive from a USB port."

"It changes nothing," Dockerty assured her.

"Sir, I—"

"You'll understand now why I didn't want you on the investigation, Inspector Craddock. How do we know Vaughan hadn't removed the hard drive himself? He could have been thinking of a new computer and didn't want to lose any of the information he had on his existing one."

Gemma backed down sheepishly. "Yes, sir."

"We need to get out there and organise these teams. Barrett, hang fire a few minutes. We're going to court. Gemma, a word in private."

He led the way from the briefing room, along the corridor and into the tiny office he had commandeered. Small, cluttered and windowless aside from one small light high on the rear wall, it was officially Gemma's office as senior CID officer.

Dockerty flounced into the chair behind the desk, Gemma sat opposite him.

"Yesterday, I specifically said that we clamp down on this case."

"Yes, sir. And?"

"Why were you speaking to Sheila Riley, Brenda Jump, Les Tanner and Sylvia Goodson in the Miner's Arms last night?"

"Because Joe will need those people over the coming weeks, especially if he's remanded in custody."

"I don't care what Joe needs. I do not want evidence in this case discussed outside this station."

Gemma's cheeks flushed. She leaned forward aggressively. "I did not discuss any evidence. If you must know, I suggested they persuade Joe to confess, and they refused because like me, they don't believe he did it."

"If you're that convinced of his innocence, why insist he should plead guilty?"

"Because unlike you, I'm willing to entertain the notion that I may be wrong."

Dockerty's colour rose. "You're walking a dangerous tightrope, Inspector."

"And so are you. Not only trying to bully your way through this case, but for the police service in Sanford as a whole. We're the ones who have to live with the flak when you go back to Leeds."

"I'm doing my job, and right now you still haven't adequately explained why you spoke to those four in direct contravention of my orders."

"Because I was concerned for Joe's welfare. They are the only people he has. He has no wife and no children. His brother lives in Australia. My cousin, Lee, and I are the nearest he can call family. After us, the only people he has in this world, the only people who can make sure he has whatever he needs while we have him locked up, are Sheila Riley, Brenda Jump, and the other members of that club he runs."

"You had better be telling it like it is. Cross me one more time, and I'll pack you off to another area until we're through here. Now get out and on with the job I allocated you."

***

After a lengthy debate with his solicitor, Paul Hagley, most of which centred on Joe's refusal to call him earlier, the magistrate's hearing began at few minutes after ten.

Led into the dock in handcuffs, Joe was not best pleased

to see the chair of the magistrates. He had had many dealings with Kenny Pemberton, the Head of Sanford Borough Council Environmental Services, few of which had been pleasant or convivial.

Before he could utter a word, however, Pemberton himself spoke up.

A pompous and overbearing man, he appeared even more so in his exalted position on the bench, and his convoluted remarks only made him appear worse to Joe.

"I feel it incumbent upon myself to make it clear to the court that I know the accused. He and I have had many an altercation in the past. If it so pleases the court, I shall step down as chair of the magistrates."

"Prat," Joe muttered under his breath.

"You must speak up if you have anything to say, Mr Murray," Pemberton said.

"You don't want to hear what I just called you."

The clerk of the court, a middle-aged woman who called at The Lazy Luncheonette occasionally, addressed Joe. "Do you have any objections to His Worship sitting as chair of the magistrates?"

"I don't care," Joe replied. "But he'll care, and so will the rest of you when I prove I didn't do it."

This led to a brief hiatus while Joe's solicitor, in hurried whispers advised him, "shut it, Joe, or they'll wall you up until Christmas."

But the damage was already done. Joe spoke only twice more. Once to confirm his name and address, the second time to enter a plea of not guilty.

Before going into their deliberations, Hagley made a plea for bail.

"My client is of previous good character, Your Worship, and he wholeheartedly denies any involvement in the crimes for which he is charged. He is also a businessman, and to remand him in custody may seriously impair the pursuance of trade and threaten the livelihood of his staff."

The bench called up Dockerty to give evidence.

"You are pursuing other lines of inquiry,

Superintendent?" Pemberton asked.

"We are, sir. I would rather not specify the direction of those inquiries, for reasons of confidentiality, but for the moment, I remain satisfied that the suspect is involved in this crime."

"Do you object to bail?"

"Not specifically, sir. The charge is murder, and the secondary charge is arson. In such circumstances it would be unusual to allow bail, and we are aware that Mr Murray's ex-wife resides in the Canary Islands. That doesn't, however, mean we would be worried about him taking flight there."

The bench went into a huddle again, quietly deliberating, calling on the clerk to the justices for guidance. At length, Pemberton looked up and fixed Joe's stare with his own.

"I'm sorry but the legal position on this is quite clear. Murder is an indictable offence, and we are happy that there is a case to answer. You will be remanded in custody for twenty-eight days, which, I should think, will give the police the time they require to gather their evidence and put forward their case."

As he was led from the dock, Joe delivered one final glare at Pemberton, a stare which skewered the magistrate and silently warned him, 'you will regret this'.

***

It was a broody Ray Dockerty who rose to greet Brad Kilburn when a uniformed sergeant showed the fire officer into the tiny office at the rear of Sanford police station.

"Thanks for coming in, Brad." Dockerty waved his visitor to the chair opposite. "You want tea, coffee or anything?"

"I'll pass, thanks, Ray." Kilburn stared around the squalid quarters. Most of the walls were bare, and the only natural light came from a small window high up on the side wall. Looking through it, all that could be seen were the bricks of the building next door.

"Not as grand as you're used to in Leeds, eh?"

Dockerty chuckled. "It's Gemma Craddock's office, really, but I have to have a place where I can marshal the troops." There was a long moment of silence while Dockerty chose his approach. "You probably know that we've remanded Joe Murray for this business, and this—" he opened the file in front of him and briefly held it up. "— is the report on the fire at the old Lazy Luncheonette. I was struck by the similarities between that and the way Vaughan's house was torched."

"Both sparked with petrol, probably unleaded, both employed cooking oil as an accelerant."

"And yet, neither Joe Murray nor Gerard Vaughan could have set the fire at the old place. They were both in Blackpool at the time, and there are too many witnesses who can vouch for that for it to be anything but the truth."

"It was an amateur job, Ray, and either of them could have paid someone to set it."

"Amateur?"

Kilburn nodded. "A professional torch would have used more elaborate means of setting the fire. Phosphorous, magnesium, even sodium gradually sinking into water, with other flammables nearby. The fire on the old Britannia Parade was laid in the supermarket next door to The Lazy Luncheonette. A couple of bricks had been knocked out and cooking oil spread across the floor of Joe's café. It was then trigged with petrol and a candle. Effective, but primitive, amateur and easy to track."

"So the report tells me," said Dockerty, who had sat patiently through the thin explanation. "But does that indicate someone who did the job on behalf of either Murray or Vaughan? Someone who worked cheaply?"

"Probably. Possibly. I don't know. That kind of investigation is your department. Our people are only concerned with the how, not the who or the why."

"I accept that, but consider my position. I'm a stranger in Sanford. The one thing I can be sure of is that half this town hates Joe Murray and the other half thinks the sun shines out of his backside. I need an absolutely unbiased opinion on some things. You've just half-agreed that either Joe or Vaughan could have paid an amateur to set the fire, but I can't understand why. Correction. I could understand why Vaughan would do it. Murray's delaying tactics were costing him a fortune. But Murray... According to my information, he was on the verge of taking a large settlement under a compulsory purchase order. All he got from his insurers was exactly the same. Possibly less because I'm not sure how much the insurers would pay him for consequential loss. What possible motive could he have for torching the place?"

Kilburn smiled weakly. "Again, that's your department, not mine, but I can say... How well do you know Joe?"

"Not that well, but our paths have crossed in the past. I know he's irritable, cantankerous, has a fairly low opinion of the police. A fairly low opinion of anyone other than himself, come to that. The only two people who appear to have any influence over him are Sheila Riley and Brenda Jump, and even then, he's troublesome."

Kilburn laughed. "That's Joe. I've known him years and to be truthful, he'd pick an argument with just about anyone, even his own reflection, purely for the sake of picking an argument. If you said to him his café is the best in Yorkshire, he'd argue that it wasn't and give you a shed load of reasons why."

"It won't do him much good in the nick." Dockerty brought his rambling mind to bear. "So what are you getting at, Brad?"

Kilburn sat forward, elbows resting on his knees, hands clasped ahead of him. For a few moments, he stared down at the hard-wearing carpet. At length he looked up and at Dockerty.

"I'm not saying this is right. In fact, it's probably totally wide of the mark, but Joe could have had the old place torched just to make mischief."

Dockerty's eyes widened. "Mischief?"

"Look at it this way. The compulsory purchase order had

been issued. Joe threatened to appeal and appeal and appeal, but he knew it wouldn't do any good. All it would do was slow the process down. The DIY shop, the minimarket, hairstylist and the laundrette had all closed and Britannia Parade was run down, on the point of falling down. It didn't matter what Joe did, the council were always going to demolish the place, and he knew that. So, he's off to Blackpool for the weekend with those muppets from the 3rd Age Club. He tells that gormless nephew of his, Lee, to set the fire over the weekend, then bell him on Monday morning acting all surprised. What's he done? He's gonna come out of it on top no matter which way it goes. Whether the CPO or his insurance company, someone is gonna pay up. But it gives him the excuse to have a serious go at Vaughan. Let's face it, Ray, Joe and Vaughan got on like water and electricity. Joe appears innocent, and Vaughan is the more likely candidate to have set the fire, and to Joe's tiny mind, he's won the argument, and he's in exactly the same position as he would be if he'd let the CPO go through."

"All a bit extreme just for the sake of winning an argument," Dockerty argued. "But then, why kill Vaughan fifteen months later?"

Kilburn shrugged. "Perhaps Vaughan found out. Maybe he called Joe to his house to confront him. That safe was empty, you know, and according to my information, the hard drive was missing out of that laptop. I don't see Joe as a safebreaker, but maybe Vaughan showed him the evidence and Joe lost it." He sat back. "I'm speculating, Ray, nothing more, and I'm probably totally wrong, but I'll tell you this. Joe's insurers hired a professional investigator to look into it. She visited me a few times, and she's spoken to Joe – and Vaughan, mind you – a fair number of times since the turn of the year."

"Do you know who she was?"

"Woman called Latham. Denise Latham."

Dockerty's face lit up in delight. "Ex-Detective Sergeant Latham? Leeds?"

"Search me. She came from Leeds, sure, but she never mentioned having been a cop."

"It's gotta be her."

"You know her, then?"

"She was on my team at one time. When I was a DI. Packed it in a few years back after she got passed over for promotion. I'll bell the insurance company and... Any idea who they are?"

"North Shires, I think."

"I'll get onto them and see what they can tell me. Thanks, Brad. You've given me something to think about."

Chapter Seven

It was pure luck that Denise Latham was not asleep at the time the loss adjusters of North Shires Insurance rang.

She had arrived home after a tiring day where she was supposedly seeking video evidence against a claimant seeking damages for an alleged accident in a large department store. The claimant insisted she was unable to walk properly after tripping and falling down an escalator. The insurance company were unhappy with the medical reports they had received, and acting on a tip off, suspected fraud. They hired Denise to monitor the claimant, and Denise was, as always, happy to take the job subject to a daily rate and a percentage of money saved. Since the claim was on the order of £50,000, she was in for a healthy pay packet once she got the evidence.

But a day spent discreetly parked outside the claimant's council home had produced absolutely nothing. The woman never set foot out of the house between Denise's arrival at ten a.m. and her departure at six p.m.

After picking up a takeaway, she went home and switched on the TV. She had already missed her favourite teatime reality shows, and the rest of the night's schedule, the other side of the news hour, did not look inviting. She left the machine talking to the empty room while she prepared the takeaway.

Returning to her modest living room, she sat at the table, and picked up the remote. About to start channel hopping in search of entertainment, the telephone rang to interrupt.

"Denise? It's Edie at North Shires. Have you got the TV on?"

"Yes. Why?"

"Whip over to the Beeb and the local news. The item should run in a few minutes. I'll bell you back after it's finished."

"Yes, but… Edie? Are you there, Edie?"

Irritated but not a little puzzled, Denise picked up the remote again, and switched channels to find a serious-faced newscaster running into the next item.

"Police in Sanford, West Yorkshire, have charged a man with the murder of Gerard Vaughan. Valerie Immingham has the story."

The scene cut from the Leeds studio to the market square in Sanford, where the reporter, looking hot in her grey business suit and plain white blouse, did her piece to camera.

"Joseph Murray, who runs a popular café here in Sanford, was arrested first thing yesterday morning, but later released. He was re-arrested yesterday afternoon when new evidence was found, and brought before Sanford magistrates this morning, where he was remanded in custody for twenty-eight days. In a brief statement, Detective Superintendent Raymond Dockerty, of Leeds CID, who is in charge of the case, said he was satisfied that they had the right man."

The scene cut away once more, this time to a shot of The Lazy Luncheonette from the opposite side of Doncaster Road, while Valerie Immingham continued her commentary voiceover.

"Joe Murray is the proprietor of The Lazy Luncheonette, a popular, lorry drivers' café on the main road out of Sanford. It's known that there was bad blood between Murray and his victim, Gerard Vaughan, after the original café burned down a year ago, an act which Murray accused Vaughan of inciting."

One more the scene cut back to the market square.

"Superintendent Dockerty refused to speculate on possible motives for the crime, but with Murray remanded to HM Prison Sanford, efforts will continue to find the evidence and build the case against him. Valerie

Immingham from Sanford, handing you back to the studio."

Snatching up the remote, Denise muted the TV, and reached for her phone. Before she could dial, it rang again.

"Denise? Edie again. So what do you think?"

"I'm on my way to Sanford in about ten minutes," Denise said.

"If the cops have him for murdering Vaughan, what price he also burned down his old place?"

"Off the top of my head, Edie, it's twaddle. Joe Murray did not burn down the old Lazy Luncheonette. Vaughan did. And Joe did not murder Gerard Vaughan."

"But—"

"Gotta go, Edie. I need to be in Sanford. I'll keep you posted."

This time it was Denise who cut the connection. Dropping the phone on the table, her takeaway forgotten, she dashed to the bedroom, dragged a pair of denim jeans and a thin top from the wardrobe and hurriedly dressed. Sanford was half an hour away on the motorway. Should she stay there or commute when she was through for the night?

Opting for the latter, she dragged on a pair of sensible, flat walking shoes and returned to the living room, where she loaded her handbag with everything she was likely to need, checked her purse to ensure she had cash and cards with her, and switched off the TV. Dropping the mobile into her bag, she all but ran from the flat. Five minutes later, she was in the car, running the engine, and dialling The Lazy Luncheonette.

Predictably, she got no answer. Next she telephoned the *Sanford Gazette* and after a brief discussion with one of the late-shift reporters, she learned that an extraordinary meeting of the Sanford 3rd Age Club had been called for eight o'clock in the upstairs rooms of the Miner's Arms.

Putting the car into gear, and releasing the handbrake, she checked the dashboard clock and read 7:15. She would be at the Miner's Arms in plenty of time.

She had spoken to Joe Murray several times after their

first meeting early in the New Year, and although he remained hostile towards her, she had nevertheless formed an opinion. There was an outside chance that he set the fire at the old place, but having also met with Vaughan on any number of occasions, her money was firmly on the property developer.

No matter who set the fire, there was not one chance in a billion that Joe Murray murdered Vaughan. Arrogant and irritable he might be, but there was a quirky sense of moral responsibility and justice about him. He would tolerate minor, civil offences, such as fly tipping, or double parking. Actions which he saw as nothing more than annoyances, often used as cash cows for the local authority and actions he was frequently guilty of himself. But when it came to true crime – burglary, mugging, robbery, assault, rape, murder and the like – he was blessed with a genuine repugnancy that compelled him to take action in an effort to bring the perpetrators to justice.

Unless Denise had misjudged him, and she did not often make mistakes, Joe Murray was incapable of murder.

And yet, as she drove east along the M62, her thoughts turned to the thoroughness of her former boss, Ray Dockerty.

Loud, often brash, Dockerty had never been a 'yes' man, but his approach to investigation was methodical and meticulous. According to the news, he had charged Joe. Did they mean charged? Or had he been remanded on suspicion? The difference may not mean much to a TV reporter, but it made all the difference in the world to the police and ultimately to Joe. He would never be able to sue for wrongful arrest if he was held on suspicion, and in any event, Dockerty would not have remanded him unless he had compelling evidence.

Her thoughts were still tumbling on these matters when she pulled onto the car park of the Miner's Arms at ten minutes to eight, and cut the engine.

The car park was busy for a Wednesday evening. A factor, she guessed, of the meeting called by Joe's deputies.

When she stepped into the lounge bar, she found it, too, was crowded. Men and women, mostly of her generation or the one before, stood shoulder to shoulder at the bar, or crowded into the corner watching some talent competition on TV, and it took her many minutes to secure a glass of lager.

She kept an eye on the clock. It would not do to turn up in the top room before the meeting had begun. She was not a member of the Sanford 3rd Age Club, and they would demand that she leave. But at eight fifteen, by which time she judged they would be in full debate, she detached herself from the packed bar, and made for the staircase.

The barman called to her before she could climb the steps. "Hey up, missus. You can't go up there. Private meeting."

Denise smiled. "Can't I? Watch me."

***

As the summer night drew in, Joe lay on his bunk in Sanford Prison and seethed at the injustice which had been heaped upon him. He was no killer, but in order to prove that he needed to be out there, not locked up in here.

Sanford was a Category C prison, designed for remand prisoners, and those who could be trusted not to try and escape, but not yet ready for the even more relaxed regime of an open prison.

Upon arrival and reception Joe was pleased to see at least one familiar face. Warder Harvey Thornton was about fifteen years Joe's junior, although his shaven head and cragged looks made him appear much older. His father had been a lorry driver and a regular at The Lazy Luncheonette.

"Not that it'll cut any ice in here, Joe," Thornton warned him. "There are rules. If you break 'em, I'll put you on report and you can lose your privileges."

"I'm innocent, Harv," Joe told him as they marched towards the cells.

"Not our problem, mate. That's between you, the courts,

your brief and the cops. We're here to stop you from buggering off to Tenerife and joining your missus."

"Ex-missus," Joe stressed as they arrived at his allocated cell.

"Here's your digs, Joe. We're short of space, so you're sharing. Neave rabbits a lot, but I'm sure you'll soon shut him up. Sheila Riley's already telephoned and arranged a visit for her and Brenda Jump tomorrow. If you need anything, you can use the phone to ring her."

"I sent instructions with my solicitor. They know what to bring."

"Right. Now remember, Joe, we're fairly easy going here, but there are rules. Cross the line and there's no negotiation. You'll be in bother."

Thornton was right about Eric Neave. From the moment Joe entered the cell, the man did nothing but talk. Almost seventy years old, his hair greyed and diminished to a light dusting on his narrow crown, he shuffled around with a stoop and a shaking hand that had Joe concerned every time the man reached his plastic, issue mug and a drink of water.

"What they got you for then?" Neave asked after giving Joe a rundown of the dos and don'ts in HMP Sanford.

In an effort to shut him up, Joe injected a degree of ice and threat into his voice. "Murder."

Neave's reply surprised him. "Yeah. Me too."

Joe switched tack immediately, but did not suppress his anger. "I'm innocent."

"Yeah. Me too."

If this response did not surprise Joe quite as much, it did provide Neave with the opportunity to begin chattering.

"Someone knifed the missus. Cops blamed me. Course it wasn't me. I was on me allotment at the time, tending the azalea bush. Do you know how hard they are to grow round here? Need a good, acidy soil. Too alkaline round here. Years I've worked on the bleeding azalea and I've got it just right and bang… the cops lock me up for summat I didn't do."

It occurred to Joe that Neave sounded more interested in

his azalea than his wife's death. "You been married long?" he asked.

"Thirty odd years. Thirty-seven, I think."

"Only you don't sound too upset that she was killed."

"Got over it, haven't I? Three months I've been in here. Waiting for me trial, and the cops ain't got nothing, you know. I never touched her. She weren't a bad old stick, Annie. Whinging cow when she wanted." Neave chuckled. "She once told me I thought more about my azalea than I did of her. I told her, I said, 'you grew up round here. You're used to the soil'." He laughed again. "Then someone ran her through with a knife. Cops said they've got other evidence, but get this, they never found the knife what did her. Reckoned I chucked it in the river, they did. Won't have it, see. Won't believe that I wasn't at home when it happened."

The lights in the cell went out, and there was a long pause. Joe was drifting off into light sleep when Neave's voice broke into the growing, summer darkness.

"Trouble is, see, that azalea won't last long unless it gets the right care and attention. And will the police do that? Will they hell as like. I got word out to one of my neighbours to look after it, but you can't rely on him. Too busy watching football on his satellite telly, he is."

Joe was trying to sleep, but Neave's words stirred something in him. Get someone to look after the plant. Get someone to look after the killing of Vaughan. Had Neave got his lazy neighbour to look after the killing of his wife? Someone so innocuous, no one would think to look there. Had Mr X got someone to look after the killing of Vaughan? Someone so innocuous no one would think to look there? Was Neave's football-mad neighbour skilled in the art of concealing his involvement? Was Mr X's contractor skilled in the art of concealing his, too, and laying it off on Joe? Had the neighbour really murdered Annie Neave, and skilfully laid it off on this man in the cell?

Joe's frustration welled again. At home, in his tiny council flat, he could have sat at the table all night, with the netbook open in front of him, and written down his thoughts, looking for those tell-tale signs, the little giveaways that would point him in particular directions. Here he had nothing. Not even a pen and paper... although he had asked that Sheila and Brenda bring him writing materials when they visited.

Instead, he had to commit it all to memory, and trust that he would not forget come the morning.

So the summer's night, never completely dark, settled on HMP Sanford, and in the remand wing, Eric Neave waffled aimlessly and endlessly on the problems of his wife's death and the fate of his azalea bush, while in the bunk above, Joe Murray drifted into a troubled and fitful sleep.

***

No one noticed Denise when she first walked into the top room of the Miner's Arms. The meeting was in full flow and it soon became obvious that Les Tanner had been appointed Chairman in Joe's absence. But the air was thick with debate, some of it angry as George Robson, recently elected shop steward for the workforce of Sanford Borough Council's Leisure Services, threatened to bring the department out on strike in support of Joe.

His announcement was greeted with catcalls, moans and groans and some irritated responses before Brenda Jump quietened the crowd down so she could be heard.

"You know how Joe feels about industrial action, George. He doesn't approve."

"Cos he's a raving, money-grabbing capitalist."

"You're a raving idiot, but nobody holds it against you," Mort Norris called out.

"Say that again, Norris, and you'll be a hospitalised market trader."

Les Tanner rapped his glass on the table. "Order, gentlemen, please." He concentrated on George. "Industrial action from a department Joe has nothing to do with, won't help. Come to that, industrial action from *any* department or company will not make the slightest bit of difference. I'm sure Joe would appreciate your show of solidarity, George, but let's stick to common sense, constructive ideas." A hand shot up in the audience, and Tanner narrowed his attention on it. "Alec?"

Alec Staines, a self-employed painter and decorator, got to his feet and half turned to address the room. "That last time this happened, Joe was slated on TV and in the press. Now I play golf with Ian Lofthouse, the editor of the *Gazette*. I can try to persuade him to come down in Joe's favour this time."

"That is the kind of thing we need," Sheila Riley declared. "Brenda and I will be visiting Joe tomorrow. We'll ensure he has everything he needs while he's on remand, and we'll make sure he has the best representation in legal terms, but it would be really helpful if any of you could vouch for Joe's movements on Monday night. Did anyone in this room see him after he left this place?"

He query was greeted with silence, and her face fell momentarily. Then her eyes focussed on Denise, and slow anger crept across her delicate features. "Ms Latham, this is a private meeting, and even if it were open to the public, you are the last person who would be welcome here."

Silence fell. To a man and woman, the whole room turned and followed the accusation in Sheila's glare.

Many of them knew Denise, but not all. Notwithstanding that, she felt a wall of hostility rushing towards her, and nervousness took hold; a nagging doubt that she had felt many times as a police officer. She drew in a breath to calm herself.

"For those who don't know," Brenda declared, "this is Denise Latham, private investigator for North Shires Insurance, and she's spent the last six months accusing Joe of burning down the old Lazy Luncheonette."

A mutter of discontent rumbled through the gathering.

"That's not strictly true, Mrs Jump," Denise said. "I've been trying to find out who started that fire, and Joe Murray is only one suspect."

"Why don't you leave now?" Brenda demanded. "While you can still walk."

Tanner tapped Brenda on the arm, and there was a whispered exchange, before he addressed Denise. "I'm sorry, Ms Latham, but whether or not you have any bias against Joe, this is a private, members-only meeting, and I must ask you to leave."

"Why don't you all calm down a minute?" Denise suggested. "I'm here to praise Caesar, not to bury him."

Sheila tutted. "Aside from an ability to misquote Shakespeare, are you saying you're no longer interested in the arsonists who burned down our old place?"

"No. I'm still looking for the culprit and it may very well be Joe. But whatever he's done, I don't believe he's a killer. I think the police have it wrong. And as an ex-police officer myself, I can probably do more good than any strikes in the parks and gardens department or a round of golf with the editor of the local rag."

Chapter Eight

Thursday morning dawned with the now-familiar cloudless skies and soaring temperatures. Facing his two senior detectives, Dockerty's face did not mirror the glorious weather.

His accusing stare fell on Barrett. "You're telling me that the search of both The Lazy Luncheonette and Murray's flat produced absolutely nothing?"

The sergeant shifted uncomfortably in his seat. "Aside from the netbook, sir, no. We went door to door with the neighbours, and no one remembers seeing Murray's car leave the area." He checked his pocketbook. "Team A did get a drum count at The Lazy Luncheonette, although I don't know what that will prove one way or the other. Twenty-one empty and three full. And forensic did take random samples from some of the empties, but the detailed analysis, and particularly the batch test Murray talked about, will take time."

Dockerty's stare swung onto Gemma, who refused to wither as Barrett had done.

"We had a report from forensic on Uncle Joe's car, sir. Under ultraviolet, they found a couple of latent footprints. Both partials, both from trainers. They're guessing the size at eleven or twelve, and they'll confirm later when they've identified the make."

"What size does Murray take?"

Gemma had no need to check her notes. "Seven, sir."

Dockerty dismissed it with an angry downward wave of one hand. "It means nothing. Murray could have had someone else driving. Hell, he could even have put on a pair of size twelves to cover his tracks. Ike, are forensic finished at the café?"

"Yes, sir."

"I'll telephone Mrs Riley. The place can open up again." He ran a hand through his thick head of hair. "I cannot believe we can't find more evidence."

"We have enough, sir," Barrett insisted.

Dockerty snorted. "We have enough for a charge, but we do not have one single piece of credible evidence to put Joe Murray at the scene of the crime, and without it, the defence would tear us to pieces. That video, for example. It's so grainy that we can't say whether or not it was Murray driving the car. His defence can and will offer alternative explanations for everything we say. The CPS wouldn't bother taking it to court. We need something to tie this man down at the scene. Something concrete. Something he can't get out of it."

"Sir—"

Dockerty held up a hand to silence Gemma before she could speak. "I've heard it before, Gemma, and I'm not interested. Joe is guilty until I see evidence to the contrary."

She sucked in a deep breath. "With respect, sir, you haven't heard it before, and I strongly object to being treated like probationer."

He pointed a quivering finger at her. "I warned Gillespie yesterday about his tone of voice when speaking to me. It applies to you too. Any more and I'll suspend you."

"Then may I suggest you show some respect for my rank and hear what I have to say. That way I don't need to come on strong."

Now Dockerty sighed. "All right. Let's hear it."

Gemma paused a moment to collect herself. "There are only two possible outcomes to our present course of action. Joe is guilty or Joe is innocent. I accept the reasons behind you barring me from the investigation, but we're only looking at one side of the coin. Suppose Joe really is innocent?"

"Gemma—"

"Hear me out, sir. Please. I'm stuck in this station with

my thumb up my bum, pottering with evidence, and even then I have to have a constable with me. I could be out there, learning about Vaughan. Is there anyone who hates him enough to murder him… aside from Joe that is? That way, *if* Joe is proven innocent, at least we might have a start on other suspects."

Dockerty drummed his fingers on the desk, his brow furrowed.

More familiar with the superintendent and his moods, Barrett chipped in. "It makes sense, sir. Murray or not, we will need to look into Vaughan and his past at some point, and if Inspector Craddock is happy to do it…" He trailed off and waited for Dockerty's decision.

"All right, we'll go for it. But I'm warning you, Gemma, if you come across anything that points to your uncle, you come away from it and report back to me. Understood?"

Gemma nodded. "Perfectly."

Dockerty swung his attention back to Barrett. "Murray told us something about the drum count. It's probably meaningless, but after what we saw on the CCTV, it could give us a line of inquiry. Does the number of drums match up with his accounts?"

"I, er, I don't know, sir. We didn't go through the accounts. We have the books, obviously. Team B found them in his apartment. But it could take days to go through them."

The superintendent shook his head. "I know a woman who'll crack it in a matter of hours. Get a courier. I want those books sent to Tara Ipson in Leeds. Get on the horn to her, tell her what we want and that it's top priority. I want an answer before the weekend. Gemma, you're the local yokel, so I'll leave it to you how you pursue inquiries on Vaughan's history. Come up with any credible alternatives and something to back up your ideas, and I promise you we will follow it up. Ike, when you've sent those accounts to Leeds, gather both teams and get back out to Eastward. Repeat the door-knocking. Someone must have seen more than a dark-coloured Ford Ka arriving there. But don't go with them. I have another job for you. You're not gonna like it, but it needs to be done."

"Sir?"

"Get out a map of Sanford. Track the possible routes from Murray's flat to the murder scene, then get onto the local authority and pinpoint every speed, traffic control and CCTV camera on those routes. It's a hell of a long shot, but if Joe's car went out there, he will have been caught on one of those cameras. I want to know where and when." Dockerty stood. "Let's get on with it."

"Where will you be, sir?"

"Talking to the press. After I've spoken with the chief super."

***

Irwin Queenan, Chief Planning Officer for Sanford Borough Council, believed in tidiness and organisation, and it was spelled out in the orderliness of his desk, and the cut of his pinstriped suits, and even the precise way his plain tie cut through the centre of his shining white shirts. He was a man for whom the minutiae mattered.

When, therefore, Les Tanner, Chief Payroll Officer, entered his office, it took Queenan by surprise.

"I don't recall our having an appointment, Les."

"We don't," Tanner replied. "This is off the record and more to do with a matter of mutual concern."

Queenan waved his visitor into a chair, one of a pair set at two o'clock and ten o'clock from Queenan's point of view. "I don't have long. Chief Executive's meeting in about half an hour."

"I have to be there, too," Tanner said, taking the offered seat.

Behind the desk, Queenan glanced through the window while he waited. A bland view of the Town Hall's rear car park did little to enervate him. At the age of fifty-six, having worked for the Council since leaving school forty years previously, he felt his loyalty and methodical plod to the upper echelons of management, warranted a superior office; one with a view over Market Square perhaps.

He bought his attention back to Tanner. He did not particularly like the man. Ex-army, ex-Territorial reserve, and an officer, Tanner had come into the Town Hall somewhere in the middle ranks, and made his way up the ladder to the position of Chief Payroll Officer. He had done so through the force of his commanding personality, and his habit of assuming control, even when the matter under discussion was no concern to him.

He was doing it now. Refusing to speak; applying the pressure of silence, and Queenan knew that the first one to speak would yield the high ground.

Tanner, however, was an expert; Queenan was not.

"So? A matter of mutual concern?"

"Joe Murray," Tanner said. "Currently on remand, suspected of murdering Gerard Vaughan."

"I fail to see what that has to with either of us."

"He's innocent, as you well know."

"In that case, he has no need to worry, does he? Forgive me, Les, but I shouldn't have thought you'd care much about that. It's no secret that there's no love lost between you and Murray."

"Wrong. Thanks to my time in the army, and my years here at the Town Hall, I'm a better administrator than Joe will ever be, and I thoroughly disapprove of the haphazard way in which he runs the 3rd Age Club. That aside, he is a friend, and I don't like to see my friends accused of crimes they have not committed." Tanner leaned forward and jabbed his index finger into the desktop. "Particularly when there are other people in this town, other people in this very building, who have a greater motive for wishing Vaughan dead."

Queenan was taken aback. He clasped his hands together, rested them on his swelling abdomen, and glanced at Tanner's lean figure. How was it that an army officer who had never seen any real action could keep so slim at his age? Queenan's gnarled fingers and knuckles spoke of advancing arthritis, and his growing belly pointed to a lack of exercise, and yet, he was at least four or five years younger than Tanner.

He was aware that almost a minute had passed since Tanner's last remark.

"Let me get this straight, Les. Are you accusing me of murdering Vaughan?"

"Of course not. However, after the disgraceful manner in which you manipulated your disciplinary hearing, your name would certainly be on the list of suspects."

Queenan almost leapt out of his seat, but his previous thoughts on the comparative fitness of Tanner when compared to himself, prevented him. Instead, he sat forward and reached the telephone. "I think we need to bring this to the attention of the Chief Executive. Don't you?"

"Do that. Go ahead, call him. I told you this is off the record, but I'm not saying anything to you that I wouldn't say to him, and eventually, when the police decide that Joe is innocent, I'll say it to them, too." Tanner waved at the telephone. "Go ahead. Make your call."

Queenan hesitated, his mind running through many scenarios, all of them worrying. He retracted his hand and sat back.

"It may interest you to know, Queenan, that as of last night, we have a professional investigator working on Joe's behalf. A former police officer. Denise Latham. I believe you've met her a time or two. She's primarily interested in the fire which burned down Joe's old place, and she doesn't believe he's guilty of murder. No doubt she'll be paying you a call." Tanner smiled sadistically "One thing I love about Joe, you know, is his need for vengeance. It's enough to scare off the local mafia." He narrowed needle-like eyes on Queenan. "And when he gets out, I've a feeling he may pay you a call too." Tanner stood up. "Think about it."

Queenan stared at Tanner's back as he left. The malevolence in his glower faded quickly as the door closed behind the Chief Payroll Officer, and turned to one of anxiety. He snatched up the telephone and hurriedly punched in the number. He needed no directory, internal or external to remind him of it.

"It's me, Irwin," he said when the connection was made. "I've just had Les Tanner in here, and we have problems."

"What sort of problems?"

Queenan spent another few minutes detailing the things Tanner had said to him. When he had finished he was greeted by near silence. Only the sounds of activity in the office he had called let him know that he was still connected.

"You know your trouble, Queenan?" said the other man. "You worry too much. Instead of crossing bridges when you come to them, you're fretting that the bridge will actually be there. Man up, and stop fretting. Joe Murray is where the law has sent him, and he's unlikely to be coming back soon. As for this bloody woman, well so what? Let her ask her questions. If she knew anything, she'd have picked up her bonus months ago."

The line went dead. Queenan slowly replaced the receiver. He felt a shade calmer. It was true that Denise Latham knew nothing, and she would need to widen the net considerably before she could learn anything.

All the same…

***

Most of the tables in the prison canteen were occupied when Joe joined Sheila and Brenda.

If the depression of the previous day was bad, his first night and morning in HM Prison Sanford had served only to exacerbate it. Accustomed to living alone, now sharing a cramped cell with the garrulous Eric Neave, he had slept only fitfully, and efforts to bring his fine mind to bear on the matter of Vaughan's murder, proved useless. Even in the small hours, Neave would wake and disturb his concentration, until he reached the point where he felt he would lose his temper, and then he could not concentrate at all for his inner rage.

"You don't have to work if you don't want, Joe," Thornton told him when he complained, "but if you like, I can arrange for you to help out in the kitchens."

"Pass," Joe replied. "I'm innocent, Harv, and I need to work on ways of proving it. I won't be able to do that in the kitchen any more than I can in the cell with Neave prattling fifty to the dozen about his bloody azalea bush."

Accommodation options, he was told, were restricted by lack of space, and in the end, he had asked and been granted permission to use the library, and he had stayed there for much of the morning.

After lunch, he was poring over a map of the old Sanford Main Colliery, which showed both surface and underground roadways, when Thornton found him again, and told him his visitors had arrived.

"They've brought some things for you," the warder said. "All been checked and accepted."

"Well let's hope Ray Dockerty's head is one of them."

Although the two women were putting on brave faces, Joe could see through the thin, forced smiles to the concern beneath. It was made plan when Sheila asked, "How are you, Joe?"

"Couldn't be better. Haven't done anything wrong, yet here I am locked up, kept safe from all those men and women who might want to skewer me."

"Take it easy, Joe," Brenda advised. "Losing the plot won't help you regain your freedom."

He sucked in a deep breath and let it out as a hiss. "You should try it sometime, Brenda. Slammed up with some nutter who talks about his bleeding azalea plant as if his life depended on it. Some of the conversations in The Lazy Luncheonette are tedious, but this guy makes us sound like we're having a party."

"I'm sure they'll get it sorted quickly," Sheila said. "We got the message from your solicitor." She passed a large carrier bag across the table. "A change of clothing, toiletries, and he asked to make sure you got an A4 writing pad and plenty of pens."

Joe nodded his thanks. "Dockerty is hell bent on pinning this on me. And if he isn't, then young Ike Barrett is. They won't even look for anyone else while they have me in the frame, and on that basis, someone has to do some thinking and investigating. If I can get my thoughts down on paper, can I leave you two to ask the questions?"

The women exchanged a pleased glance. "We may not need to, Joe. We have help. A professional."

"Professional? Not Gemma, is it?"

"Gemma is barred from the investigation as we understand it. She's working on the periphery." Sheila smiled encouragingly. "It's Denise Latham."

Joe's eyes widened. "Denise Latham?" His malleable features sank. "That's it. I'm doomed. I may as well throw the towel in now and look forward to the next twenty-five years in here."

"Now, Joe—"

He cut in before Brenda could say more. "Can I remind you that Denise Latham has spent the last six or seven months trying to pin the fire at the old Lazy Luncheonette on me? Can I further remind you that the North Shires Insurance Company is trying to get back that quarter of a million quid they paid out, and Denise Latham is on a sizeable cut as a bonus if she can nail the culprit? I need her help like I need someone turning up with photographs of me setting fire to Vaughan's place."

"She turned up at the meeting last night and we spoke to her at some length afterwards," Sheila insisted. "We're convinced that she's trying to help."

"Well, all I can say is you must be a salesman's dream if you're that easy to fool."

Brenda tutted, but Sheila glowered and accompanied her fiery eyes with a warning. "I appreciate you're under some stress, so I'll overlook that remark… this time."

Joe took a moment to calm down, after which he demanded, "How can you be sure she's not simply out to secure her bonus?"

"She still believes you may have burned the old place

down, Joe. Although she does say Vaughan was the real favourite, but she does not believe you're a killer."

"And seeing you walled up for murder won't get North Shires their money back," Brenda added. "She needs to *prove* you set fire to the old place."

"I didn't set fire to it. I didn't set fire to Vaughan's either, and I didn't kill him."

Sheila was hesitant as she spoke next. "Joe, er, we obviously believe you're innocent, but we do have to ask this. Had Vaughan been in touch hinting that there had been a change of policy at Ballantyne's?"

"No." Joe frowned. "What are you talking about? Do you know something I don't?"

"It was something Les mentioned the other night," Brenda explained. "He wondered whether Ballantyne's had decided to drop their property holdings, and the business had reverted back to Vaughan, which would mean he could pressure you into getting out."

"And that would give me the motive for killing him." Joe snorted. "Get bloody real, will you. I know of no change of ownership, and if you don't believe me, speak to Sir Douglas or his son."

"We tried," she said. "But Sir Douglas is on holiday in Barbados, and Toby is at a conference in Geneva."

"Blooming typical. I'm rotting to hell in here, and help is thousands of miles away."

"You have us, Joe," Sheila reassured him.

Brenda smiled. "And Denise Latham."

Reminded of the information they had given him, he said, "All right. Let's play along with her. If she's out to get me, she'll let slip somewhere along the line, and anyway, there isn't much I can do in here." Reaching into the bag Sheila had given him, he took out the A4 notepad, and a pen, attracting Thornton's immediate attention.

"Careful what you're scribbling down, Joe."

"Just a note for the escape committee," Joe reassured him with a weak smile. "It's no secret, Harvey. You can read it when I'm done."

"As long as it's above board."

Sheila watched him walk away. "I thought you were allowed more privileges when you're on remand."

Joe nodded as he wrote. "Yes, but I don't have carte blanche. For all he knows, I might really be writing down instructions for my escape, or orders for you to get rid of the evidence. Make sure they see it as you leave."

He continued to write for several minutes. Eventually, he put down the pen and turned the paper for them to read while he went through it.

"The only evidence Ray Dockerty has are a couple of stills from the security cameras around Britannia Parade, and the traces of cooking oil in the boot of my car."

"And he remanded you on that?"

"Plus the knife and Joe's pen at the scene of the crime," Sheila pointed out. "Plus, Joe lives alone so there is no one to substantiate his whereabouts. Plus a witness who saw the car at or near the fire. Plus—"

"Have you thought of standing for the prosecution, Sheila?" Joe interrupted.

"I'm sorry, Joe, I was only pointing it out."

"Right. Well now that you've pointed it out, let me add something. Not one of those things *proves* that I was anywhere near Eastward on Monday night. To that end, everything Dockerty has is circumstantial. We all know I'm innocent…" He eyed them suspiciously. "We do know I'm innocent, don't we?"

Brenda grinned. "You did dump that chip fat on the fields behind The Lazy Luncheonette in 1993, Joe."

"Fry tipping," Sheila chuckled.

"All right, all right."

"Of course we know you're innocent, Joe," Sheila stressed. "So go on with what you were saying."

"Someone is trying to frame me. The video stills clearly show my car, or one that looks like it and has the same registration, turning up at the back of The Lazy Luncheonette on Monday night about half an hour after the fire is supposed to have started. They also show someone getting out of that car, cutting off the locks on the recycling shed, opening it and dumping a cooking oil drum in there. It's too hazy to see who it is, but I know it's not me."

"So where is all this leading?" Brenda asked.

"Two things. First, I was back at The Lazy Luncheonette just after six. I'd been to the wholesaler's on the retail park. There were two truckers parked overnight in the back lane. Denise should chase them up first."

"Do you know which companies?"

"Nope," Joe replied, "But there are plenty of trucking forums on the web. If she puts up enough notices, someone might come back."

"A long shot, Joe."

"But a good one if she can come up with the goods. They may have noticed something."

"You said there were two things," Brenda pointed out.

"My car key. It doesn't matter how you look at it, the killer had a key to my car. If he stole the car and then brought it back later, I wouldn't know the difference, but he would need a chipped key to start the engine. One that was programmed to turn off the immobiliser."

"If your car is on that video, he must have stolen it," Sheila objected.

"No. He could have used a look-alike. A ringer. But even then, he would have needed a key to my car to plant the oil in the boot. That is the easier option from his point of view. The correct key will open the boot, even if he can't start the car with it. Either way, he needed a key. So where the hell did he get it from?"

"Utters," Brenda suggested. "Frank never asks too many questions when he's cutting keys, does he?"

"He's one, for a start," Joe agreed, "but there are other scroats in this town who'll do it too. If Denise is serious, get her to trawl round them. Finally, she needs to speak to my neighbours. Did anyone see my car moving or missing from its parking spot at any time on Monday night?"

Sheila folded the sheet of paper and slipped it in her handbag. "None of this gets us closer to who did kill

Vaughan."

"We can worry about that when I'm out."

***

Even with the windows down and sunroof open, the interior of Denise's car felt like a hothouse. There was not a breath of wind moving through the still, sweating air, and she passed most of the hour sat outside Sanford prison wishing Sheila and Brenda would hurry up.

The only positive to come out of the Sanford 3rd Age Club meeting the previous night had been the appointment of Les Tanner as Chair in Joe's absence, and that had happened before Denise's arrival. The ensuing hour had been no more than hot air delivered by voluble members, such as George Robson, usually with agendas which they were quite happy to tag onto the problem of Joe Murray's incarceration. Denise had attended many such meetings in her time as a police officer. Meetings where, for example, ideas for recruiting more officers from ethnic minorities were diverted by efforts to allow more time off during public holidays by the use of Community Support Officers. As in the case of the Sanford 3rd Age Club, such meetings came to no conclusions.

The hour from 9:30 to 10:30, when she sat in the lounge bar with Sheila and Brenda, had been much more productive.

The two women were hard to persuade, and Denise could understand that.

"We two and Joe have been friends since primary school," Sheila had pointed out.

"You've known him six months," Brenda weighed in. "And during that time, you've caused him a lot of stress. Why should we trust you?"

Denise held her hands apart. "I freely admit that my main concern is pinning down the culprit of the original fire. However, I knew your husband, Mrs Riley... slightly. I was a detective constable in Leeds when he was an inspector

97

here, and if he were alive, I'm sure he would have vouched for me. I had to be tough. All coppers have to be. But I'm honest and I don't like to see an innocent man in jail. I know Joe is innocent. The trouble is, I only know it intellectually. I can't prove it. If you'll let me help, I may be able to prove it."

Eventually, she had won them over, and when they parted company, just after half past ten, it was with agreement that she would meet them outside Sanford prison while they visited Joe and put the proposition to him.

After a tiresome journey from Leeds (there had been one of those inexplicable delays on the motorway where no apparent cause ever materialised) she arrived on the prison car park a few minutes ahead of Sheila's Fiat, and there had been a couple of minutes of discussion before they went in.

That was almost an hour ago, and Denise had spent the time alternating between the stifling heat of the car's interior and the equally stifling heat of the exterior. She had run the engine and air-conditioning, but while the car was stationary, even that struggled to combat temperatures which, according to the news, were hotter than downtown Madrid.

It was with some relief that she saw the general flux of visitors begin to emerge from the prison, and amongst the thin crowd were Joe's friends.

Denise climbed out of the car to greet them, and Sheila handed her Joe's note.

After reading through it, Denise chewed her lip for a moment. "Car key is going to be difficult. Nothing to say our man didn't go to a cutter in Wakefield or Leeds, but I'll start with Sanford and see if anything comes up. The video, on the other hand, is a different matter. I'll have a word with the security people at Britannia Parade, and see if I can get a copy."

Sheila frowned. "Surely the police will have taken away all copies."

"They think," Denise laughed. "Leave that to me, Sheila. You'd be surprised what flashing a bit of leg and a smile of promise can do."

Brenda echoed the laugh. "It wouldn't surprise me."

"The pair of you are totally incorrigible." Sheila concentrated on Denise. "What happens from here?"

"I'll get on with what I have to do. If I can get the video I'll run through it tonight, at home. Is The Lazy Luncheonette open again?"

"The police rang me this morning," Sheila reported. "Forensic have finished their work, and we're allowed to open, but there's a lot of cleaning to be done, and that will take the rest of today and most of tomorrow. You won't believe how difficult it is to get rid of the powders and solvents they use. I don't see us opening again until Saturday, possibly even Monday."

"Fine. I'll meet the two of you there tomorrow morning about ten o'clock. For now, I'm going to call on security at Britannia Parade. I'll get onto the keys tomorrow and check the truckers' forums from home."

Chapter Nine

By the middle of Friday afternoon, after one of the busiest twenty-four hour periods she could recall, Denise was almost wishing she had never become involved.

After leaving Sheila and Brenda, she had called back at Britannia Parade and it had not taken long to learn that Todd Henshaw had been employed as a security officer since the new building first opened.

Tucked away in a windowless, ground floor office, and surrounded by CCTV monitors covering all aspects of the building both inside and out, Todd was content to let her disturb him, and like most people, he was only too happy to talk about himself.

"Lorra experience, y'see. Been in security work since I left school over twenty years ago, so I was a natural for this job."

As skilled at listening as she was talking, Denise wore a fixed smile as she sat through his chatter.

Tall, but stocky, aged about forty, his head shaven close, but with sufficient stubble to show off a thinning crown, he told her how he had wanted to join the police, but one or two minor convictions in his teens had scotched the plan, and he had settled, instead, for security work. But he complained about the pay and conditions which meant he was often called upon to work twelve-hour shifts.

Gradually, Denise brought the conversation round to the previous Monday night.

"Yeah. The cops took away sets of recordings from the CCTV cameras. Looks like they've got Joe painted right into a corner."

"Yes, well, I'm not so sure. There are things which don't

add up." Denise hastened on before Todd could ask what things. "Joe was telling me there were two truckers parked in the back lane all night."

"There was," Todd agreed. "They're a pain, those truckers, but the lane is common land, see. Belongs to the council. And it's an official parking area, so we get a few of 'em spending the night there. Can't do nowt about it. But some of 'em don't half leave a mess behind."

Changing the subject again, Denise asked, "You didn't see Joe's car turn up or him getting out and going to his recycling cupboard? It only turned up on the CCTV?"

Todd shrugged. "Locked in here when you're on nights, aren't you? We're not allowed to leave the control centre." He threw out a sweeping hand which took in the array of monitors. "Everything is on camera. It's like Big Brother. No one can get in or out without you, theoretically, knowing about it. At some stage anyone coming into the building will be caught on one of the cameras. Those in the back lane will be caught anyway, cos the cameras are fixed. All we can do is alter the zoom, and when Joe's car came in and stopped at the back of the caff, there was no need to zoom in, was there? I knew it was his car. I recognised it. And he has every right to go in his cupboard, so why should I go poking my nose in."

"It didn't occur to you that it might be someone else?"

"It was Joe's car, I'm telling you. Everyone knows his car. Besides, why would anyone break into that cupboard? There's nowt in there besides old drums and boxes and stuff. It's not like Joe keeps cash or valuables in there, and you can't get into the caff that way. No. It was Joe, or maybe Lee, and if it was Lee, then Joe sent him."

Denise considered her approach, and opted for blunt. "Can I see this footage, Todd?"

He shuddered, hunched himself back in his chair, his shoulders shrugging, head turning one way, then the other. He reached for his beaker and found it empty, then glanced over his shoulder to the kettle on a stand behind him.

Denise waited patiently for him to reply, and when he

did, his response was predictable.

"It's not me, see. It's the filth. I mean, they took copies of that stuff, y'know, and they said we're not supposed to even look at it no more, never mind show it anyone else."

"But you have seen it?"

"Oh, yeah. Course I have. I mean, I was here when the sergeant took a copy."

"So the recording is digital, Not DVD?"

He snorted. "Who uses DVD these days?"

Denise switched tack so suddenly that it took Todd by surprise. "What made you say that if it wasn't Joe, it was Lee?"

"Well… I… er…"

"It was something you spotted in the recording, wasn't it?"

Todd shook his head. "No. not really. Listen, if my gaffer knew I was even having this conversation, he'd—"

Denise cut him off. "Forget your boss, Todd, and let's think about you. I used to be a cop, you know, and they teach you the signs to look out for. The signals you're giving out tell me that you noticed something when you were watching that footage. Now if that footage can show that Joe is innocent, then you're guilty of not telling the police. Withholding evidence, it's called."

"No way. I'm not saying nowt of the kind. Joe was driving that car."

"But it could have been Lee. You said so."

"No. I said if it wasn't Joe then it *had to be* Lee. He's the only other bloke who would be driving Joe's car. And if it was Lee, then he was doing it cos Joe told him to."

Denise did not believe him, but she was getting nowhere, so once more, she altered her approach slightly. "Right, Todd, here's what I want." She dipped into her bag and came out with a memory stick. "A copy of the relevant footage, from just before the time Joe's car arrived until it left again."

"Never in a million years. No way. Can't do it. Cops said I can't and my gaffer will go with what they say. If they find

102

out, I'm done for."

"How long do you think you'll get when they learn you're suppressing evidence in a murder case?"

His colour drained, his eyes widened.

"You see, Todd, when I'm through here, if I don't get what I'm looking for, I go to Joe's lawyers, and they will come in like the Parachute Regiment."

"But the cops—"

"Are irrelevant. Before any trial, they must declare all their evidence to the defence team, and when it proves Joe innocent, everyone gets it in the neck… including you for not telling the cops what you'd noticed. And you know what CID are like. They'll pin the blame on the easiest target. You." She placed the memory stick on the worktop, alongside his computer mouse, then took out her purse. "I'll tell you summat else, Todd. I'm not asking you to do this just from the goodness of your heart, or even to save your worthless neck. I'm happy to pay you for it." She pulled out a twenty. "A bit of beer money."

The implicit, if genial threat, coupled to the money, swayed Todd, and ten minutes later, Denise climbed into her car for the twenty-mile journey home, carrying a copy of the relevant recordings, which she spent most of the evening and night watching.

The first thing she learned was that of the two trucks parked in Back Britannia Parade, one bore a Turkish registration. The other was registered to a company in the southwest, and she promptly contacted them to see whether their driver had noticed anything that night. They promised to get back to her.

She then turned her attention to the footage of Joe's car arriving, stopping outside the recycling shed, the driver getting out, cutting off the old lock, putting the drum in the cupboard and putting a new lock on before driving away. She had views from both cameras (one at either end of the building) but they told her nothing. The car registration could be made out with sufficient magnification and there was no doubt that it was Joe's car, or a more than reasonably accurate facsimile. But at neither end could the driver's face be made out and for the thirty seconds or so that the driver was out of the car, the images were taken on such a wide angle that only the body outline could be seen. Even on the highest magnification, the resolution was so blurred that no distinguishing features were visible.

And yet, she remained convinced that Todd Henshaw had seen something which persuaded him that the driver could be Lee, not Joe.

While Joe spent a further disturbed night in Sanford prison, Denise spent an equally frustrating one at home, and on Friday morning, with no response from the trucking company, and no further forward on the video front, after calling at The Lazy Luncheonette to bring Joe's friends up to date, she began the trawl of key cutters in Sanford.

She eventually arrived back at The Lazy Luncheonette just after three in the afternoon, and she had little to report.

"Just one man admits he cut a key for a Ford Ka," she told Sheila and Brenda. "Utters. He has a stall in the indoor market. He recalls cutting a key but he also recalls who had it cut... Joe."

Busy mopping the kitchen floor, Sheila clucked. "That will be when the spare key disappeared a few weeks ago. It fell off the hook on the kitchen wall into the waste bin and got thrown out with the day's rubbish."

Denise feigned interest. "Does it happen often?"

"Too often," Brenda replied. "I'm surprised we haven't lost more keys. And Joe was fuming over it. The new key cost him the thick end of eighty pounds."

"Well, the way things are going, he has a lot more to worry about than the cost of new car keys. I have to admit, I'm not hopeful. I swear this Henshaw man knows more than he's saying, but whatever it is that persuaded him it might be Lee on that recording, has escaped me, and that, girls, is about the only chance we have of getting Joe out of jail."

***

104

If Denise had her concerns, she was not alone. Across town, Dockerty sat with Tara Ipson and could not believe what he had just been told.

"You're sure?" Concern was etched into the superintendent's brow.

Seated the other side of the desk, Tara nodded slowly, her long, black hair flowing in front of her eyes when her head bowed, and back again when she raised it.

Her pale skin, which contrasted sharply with her jet black hair, sallow eyes and cheeks, reminded Dockerty of Morticia Addams. He found it almost impossible to guess her age, but he estimated it as anywhere between thirty and forty. Bits of her, particularly the strong legs exhibited beneath the hem of a tight mini-dress, made her look younger, but the crow's feet around her eyes, partly hidden by thick-framed, designer glasses, would convince anyone that she was older.

Whatever her age, she had been with the police service a long time, and she was a top-drawer, forensic accountant. No one could hide a penny but what she would find it. When she said the drum tally at The Lazy Luncheonette did not match up with the records, then Dockerty really had no business asking if she was sure.

"There should be twenty-three drums on site according to my calculations based on the accounts," she said. "Yet your boys counted twenty-four: twenty-one empty and three full. Murray's accounts, for obvious reasons, don't differentiate between full and empty, but his stock records do, and there are itemised invoices for purchases and receipts for empties when the recycling man has collected the drums. So it was a case of cross-checking, drums purchased with drums recycled, and the balance came to twenty-three. He has one empty drum too many."

Her voice was husky and seductive, and caused Dockerty to wonder about her again. Did she have a husband, a partner? Was it put on as an invitation or was it simply the result of too many cigarettes?

He mentally shook himself out of the idle and

105

inconsequential speculation. Unlike many of his peers and colleagues, he was happily married and had been so for over two decades, and he recognised this mental meandering as an involuntary means to taking his attention away from matters which confounded him.

"Murray's accounting is accurate, but it isn't simple," Tara went on. "In fact, it's a bit haphazard and it took me all of yesterday to find every entry, and double check them. When I got the figures, I thought I had it wrong, so I went through it all again, and got the same answer. Then I passed it over to Quincy... Er, you know my junior?"

"I've met him," Dockerty said, with the vague notion that the man's full name was something bizarre like Quincy Enright.

"I told him nothing and I didn't give him my results. I just told him what to look for. He spent most of this afternoon going through them, and he got the same result as me. Twenty-three accounted for, twenty-four on site." She shrugged. "I don't know what it means, Ray."

Dockerty was in the same position. "What the hell is he playing at?" he murmured loud enough for Tara to hear.

"Sorry, but psychology, I don't do. I prefer numbers. They can be made to lie, but by and large, they tell the truth, and if you know how to work with them, the lies are soon uncovered."

Dockerty smiled thinly. "You make me wish I was an accountant."

"It's not as boring as people are led to believe. My job certainly isn't." After a momentary pause while she appeared to be gathering her thoughts, she went on, "Y'see, boss, if someone tries to hide a few thou, I'll find it. He'll make a mistake somewhere in his cross-referencing, and I'll dig it out eventually. But in this case, your suspect hasn't tried to hide any money. If anything, he's sold himself short. He gets three pounds per drum from the recycler, so he's dropped three pounds on his bookkeeping. Trivial sum, sure, and I guess his intention was never to cook the books, but why has he done it?"

Dockerty reached for the phone. "That, Tara, is what I intend to find out." He jabbed at the number pad and waited for the connection to be made. "Gemma? It's Ray. Get Sergeant Barrett and bring him along to my office, will you... Yes, right now." He dropped the phone and smiled his gratitude at his visitor. "Thanks, Tara. You've opened up a can of worms, I think, and I'm not sure where it takes us, but your efforts are appreciated."

She stood up and smoothed down her dress. "No problem, boss. Can I go back to Leeds now?" Without waiting for an answer, she collected her belongings and walked out as Gemma and Ike Barrett arrived.

The superintendent greeted them both with a grunt and waved at the chairs opposite.

"We have a problem." He declared. "The drum count doesn't tally."

From her face, Dockerty could tell that Gemma's heart sank.

"He's missing one?" she asked.

"Just the opposite," Dockerty replied. "There is one drum too many at The Lazy Luncheonette."

Gemma's face lit up, and Barrett's screwed into a frown.

"He's joshing us, sir. Leading us by the nose. Confusing the issue. I mean—"

Dockerty held up his hand. "All in good time, Ike. Let me spell it out to you first."

He passed the next ten minutes detailing the things Tara had pointed out to him. When he had finished, he turned not to Barrett, but Gemma as the senior officer. "Your opinion?"

Her unequivocal answer came quickly. "Someone has gone to a lot of trouble to set Joe up, sir, and they've made the kind of mistake we need to put us on the right track."

She was going to say more, but Dockerty had already turned his attention to Barrett. "Ike?"

"It's still Murray, for me, sir. He's a clever man. We know that. All he's trying to do is muddy the issue."

"To what end?" Gemma asked.

Barrett was as definite as Gemma had been. "At some

stage, we let him go and we continue to look elsewhere. He's got away with it."

Gemma addressed the superintendent. "I disagree, sir. If Joe really had done it, he would have had more sense than to go back to his café that night to hide a drum. The car we caught on tape is a ringer."

"I was tempted to think the same, Gemma," Dockerty agreed, "but you're overlooking one thing. How did the traces of oil and a drum get into his car? Joe, himself, admitted he never carries old drums in the car."

Both subordinates tried to speak at once, but Dockerty talked over them.

"As matters stand, we have more evidence pointing at Joe than pointing any other way. Most of it is circumstantial, and this drum business is puzzling. But I'm not going to ask for his release. Not while we're in such a state. You, Gemma, are in favour of Joe's innocence, you, Ike, are against. That's the perfect position for what I want done."

"Sir?"

"Sir?"

"Don't let this get personal between the two of you. I know you by reputation, Gemma, and you are an excellent officer. Ike, I've worked with you longer than I care to remember, and you, too, are one of the best. So I don't want you falling out over a professional disagreement. Instead, I want you both to go down to The Lazy Luncheonette, and count the drums."

"Surely that's a job for a couple of uniformed constables?" Barrett protested.

"Normally, I would say yes, but we're involved in a murder hunt, Ike, and we need to get this right. There is the slightest chance that someone miscounted the drums on Tuesday. I doubt it, but I want you both there to check and double check the numbers. The reason I'm sending you two is because of your opposition on Joe's guilt. You're not going to add a non-existent drum to back up your uncle, Gemma, and you, Ike, are not going to miss one to incriminate him. You go out there, you count the drums individually. Not together. You compare the results only when you're finished. Understood?"

While agreeing, Gemma pointed out, "Sir, the café's shut, isn't it?"

"It was cleared to reopen yesterday morning. If it's still closed, you know Mrs Riley and Mrs Jump, don't you? You can ring them and have them let you in." Satisfied that Gemma was all right with the plan, Dockerty laid extra stress on his next words. "You report on this matter to me and no one else. Not the station canteen, not the *Sanford Gazette,* and not Don Oughton. Me. Right? Get on with it."

***

At The Lazy Luncheonette, Sheila, Brenda and Denise were enjoying a cup of tea and on the point of calling it a day when the two detectives arrived.

"Good afternoon, Gemma, Sergeant Barrett," Sheila greeted them. Without sounding too bitter, there was no warmth or welcome in her voice. "What can we do for you?"

"Come to hammer a few more nails in Joe's palms?" Brenda demanded. She was bitter and made no effort to hide it.

Gemma addressed Sheila. "We need to count the cooking oil drums, Mrs Riley."

Denise laughed harshly. "Oh boy, Ray Dockerty really has you at the core of this investigation, doesn't he? What's wrong? Didn't he trust uniformed to be able to count that far?"

Barrett sneered openly. "Ex-Detective Sergeant Latham. Dare I ask what you're doing here? Still chasing your bonus from the insurance company?"

"I'm doing your job, Barrett. Trying to prove who killed Gerard Vaughan. And yes, it is for my bonus from North Shires. Because I reckon whoever murdered him set that fire."

Barrett shrugged. "Joe Murray."

"Not Joe Murray," Denise retorted. "Not that you silly sods can see that. But I will, and when I do, I'll wipe that smirk off your face." Her insistent stare took in both officers. "I have a whisper that the man seen climbing out of that car on Monday night was not Joe. If that's so, then you have no case against him."

"What whisper?" Barrett demanded.

"You'll get to know when I follow it up."

"Ms Latham," Gemma said, "your history as a CID officer obliges me to be polite, but it also obliges you to understand the severity of withholding evidence. If you know something, then you must tell us, and if you don't, I'll take you in under caution."

Denise held out her hands, wrists together. "It's fair cop, guv. Slap the bracelets on me." She laughed. "You'll make a good inspector, maybe even a chief inspector or superintendent one day, Gemma, but don't try it with an old hand. I don't know anything. I've had a hint, that's all. And I'll be looking into it tonight and maybe over the weekend. If you take me in, you'll only get the same answer, so don't waste your time or mine. Just go count your drums."

Gemma sniffed haughtily. "We'll need the key for the outside storage shed, Mrs Riley."

"You know where it hangs, Gemma," Sheila replied, pointing to the kitchen. "May I ask why you need to count the drums again?"

"We're not allowed to tell you," Barrett replied, and followed Gemma into the kitchen area and then out through the rear door.

Brenda looked to Denise. "Can you guess why they need to recount them?"

"Something's wrong," Denise replied. "It's the only explanation. But quite how it ties in with everything, I don't know."

They whiled away the next five or ten minutes with chatter centred on forthcoming summer holidays, and when the two detectives returned it was obvious from the dark looks that they had found something wrong, and had probably disagreed over it.

"Well don't keep us in suspenders," Denise said. "What's wrong."

Barrett began, "I told you—"

Gemma cut him off. "There's one empty drum too many."

The sergeant glowered at her. "Superintendent Dockerty's orders were that it was not to be discussed with anyone other than him."

"I don't care about Superintendent Dockerty's orders," Gemma snapped, "and just remember who you're speaking to, Sergeant." She turned to the three women. "When Joe called at that shed on Monday night, he put the empty drum in there and it threw his figures out."

"It wasn't Joe," Brenda insisted.

"I appreciate your loyalty, Mrs Jump, but the fact remains—"

Sheila, who had bitten her tongue since the two offices arrived, cut Gemma off and finally let rip. "The fact remains, Gemma, that you are coming across holes in your theories and you're trying to make them fit what you see are the facts, rather than admitting that you have it wrong. As far as I'm concerned, that is disgraceful."

"Please, Mrs Riley," Barrett begged. "We're trying to get to the truth."

"You wouldn't know the truth if it smacked your bare backside," Sheila ranted.

Brenda took up the cause. "Joe may be the grumpiest man in Sanford. He may even be the most tight-fisted man in Sanford, but he is not a fool. His records are never so much as one penny out. I know. I worked in banking for years, and I've checked his books often enough. If Joe really had carried out this crime, he would not be stupid enough to make that kind of mistake. You have the wrong man. What will it take for you to admit it?"

Gemma shrugged. "Proof."

"I am sick of the way my orders are ignored," Dockerty yelled when Gemma and Barrett faced him half an hour later. "I told you not to discuss the matter with anyone, and that included the two women at The Lazy Luncheonette."

"And I am sick of the way we are told to shut up in an effort to paper over the cracks," Gemma retorted. "Mrs Riley and Mrs Jump are right. Joe is not a fool. If he'd done this, you wouldn't have found a single trace of him, and he certainly wouldn't have been stupid enough to throw an empty drum into that shed, knowing that it would put his accounting out of joint. And that's assuming he was stupid enough to use his own car, knowing it would be caught on the building security cameras. And even then we're assuming he'd be so gormless as to go anywhere near The Lazy Luncheonette after murdering Vaughan and setting fire to the man's house. You locked up the wrong man because someone intended you to do just that."

Simmering on the edge of another explosion, Dockerty pointed a shaking finger at her. "You get out there, Inspector, and prove it. Until you can, I don't want to see you again."

Gemma leapt to her feet. "Fine by me. But when I do prove it, I will do everything I can to expose what's been going on here. I'll throw my warrant card in and go public on the matter if I have to."

Gemma stormed from the office and Dockerty ran that same, shaking hand through his hair.

"What do we do is she's right, sir?"

"Find a set of dentures tough enough to eat the humble pie."

Back at The Lazy Luncheonette, the three women were ready for locking up and making their separate ways home.

Waiting for Sheila and Brenda to discard their working

clothes, Denise admired the line of photographs on the wall.

"Joe had his casebooks on shelves in the old place," Sheila commented. "All the crimes he's solved over the years. But they went up with the building and he hasn't got round to having them reprinted, so he put those photos up."

"You look like a happy crew," Denise said.

"We were until this lot blew up," Brenda said, joining them. She reached out to straighten the photograph of them and Joe stood by his car. "He's Napoleon, the tiny tyrant, and we're Wellington's army."

Denise did not answer, she was staring intently at the picture Brenda had just reset. "That's Joe's car?" she asked.

"Yes. That's the infamous Ford Ka which was caught—"

"Sheila, Brenda, can I take that picture with me?"

The request caught the two women by surprise.

"I don't know," Sheila said. "Joe wouldn't be too keen on —"

"I think it may prove his innocence."

Sheila and Brenda exchanged one of their glances.

"How?" Brenda asked.

"I won't know unless I can take it home. Trust me, I'll bring it back to you by Monday morning."

Brenda unhooked it from the wall. "Take it. But if it gets damaged, we'll blame you."

Denise barely passed to smile as she hurried through the kitchen to the back lane. "If I'm right, he won't give a damn."

The twenty-mile journey home, through the worst of the Friday rush hour, was a nightmare for Denise. She urgently needed to be back in her apartment taking prints from the CCTV footage, but the pressure of traffic was such that even on the motorway, she found herself travelling at an average of 10mph in stop-start queues stretching as far as she could see.

It was turned five when she finally rushed into her apartment. Even before kicking off her shoes, she booted up the computer and the printer/scanner beneath it. While waiting for them to go through their start routines, she moved to the kitchen and made a cup of tea. By the time she returned, everything was ready.

The first task was to run the CCTV footage and take several snapshots out of it. When that was done, she put them into a photographic enhancement package, and enlarged them. While the printer began to slowly churn them out, she removed the photograph of Joe and the two women stood alongside his car, from its frame and placed it on the scanner glass.

The A4 sized images took an age to print. The moment they were done, she opened the scanner software and enlarged the photograph from the café to the same size, and only when that was printed off, did she finally began to relax. Comparing the two images, she felt a surge of excitement and not a little pride, rush through her. She was right she even took a ruler to prove it.

Feeling elated, she snatched up the phone and dialled.

"Superintendent Dockerty, please," she asked after announcing herself.

"I'm sorry, Ms Latham, but he's gone home for the weekend."

"Get a message to him. I'll see him at Sanford police station first thing in the morning. If he's not there, I'll speak to Superintendent Oughton instead, and if neither of them are there, I'll speak to the press and TV."

Chapter Ten

Ever since his rise to the higher ranks, Dockerty had made a point of not working over the weekend unless circumstances forced him.

With the news that an old colleague had demanded to see him on pain of going over his head or worse, speaking to the media, he made an exception and was at the station for just after nine on Saturday morning. When Denise entered the tiny back room, and put her briefcase on the floor, he greeted her with a broad smile. "Detective Sergeant Latham. How the hell are you?"

Sitting opposite, placing her briefcase on the floor beside her, she wagged a pleasant, scolding finger at him. "*Former* Detective Sergeant Latham, and I'm fine, thanks, Ray."

"I always said it was a sad day for Leeds CID when you packed it in."

She shrugged. "What can I say? Sex discrimination as far as I was concerned. I dotted all the I's, crossed all the T's, passed my exams, and they still promoted others over my head."

"Treading on the chief super's toes so often didn't do you any favours, Denise. I think the idea of you as an inspector terrified him."

"You're a fine one to talk. How many times did you backchat him? How many rows did you have with him?" She grinned. "You still made it to superintendent, though."

"I gave them an ultimatum. Either promote me, or I move to the Met. Did your claim of constructive dismissal pass muster?"

With a shrewish grimace, she shook her head. "Still going on. Over two years now."

"And while you wait for possible reinstatement, you're fooling around trying to recoup money for insurance companies?" He laughed. "Considering your arrest record with the police, it must be like cleaning up after the party and picking up loose change."

"Don't knock it until you've tried it, Ray. I make more now than I ever did as a cop, and I'm my own boss. The insurance companies don't worry about trivia like the Police and Criminal Evidence Act. All they need is *prima facie* evidence, which I supply, and their lawyers go in like the SAS."

"Hence the threats I got by phone." Dockerty became more serious. "I'd expect better of you, Denise. What is so important that I have to drag my backside down here on a Saturday?"

"Joe Murray and The Lazy Luncheonette."

Dockerty groaned. "Not you, too. Look, Denise, I don't know whether Joe Murray had a hand in burning down the old building, and I don't care."

"I'm not here about the old Lazy Luncheonette. I can imagine Joe burning it down, but considering the compulsory purchase settlement which was on the table at the time, it's difficult to see what he would gain from it. I think it's more likely that Gerard Vaughan did it, but he's not gonna admit it now, is he?"

"So if not for your clients, why are you here?"

"Because you have Joe locked up for Vaughan's murder. I've got to know him over the last few months, Ray, and he's no killer."

"I thought I'd had enough of this from his niece." He sighed. "I wouldn't have thought so either, but the evidence says different."

Denise bent, picked up her briefcase, settled it on her knee and flipped it open. "And if I show you evidence that you're wrong? Will that help?"

The genial façade Dockerty had been wearing since she entered, disappeared quickly to be replaced by the darker, more business-like front of the professional police officer.

"What evidence?"

From the case, Denise took her enlargement of the photograph from The Lazy Luncheonette. Laying it on the desk, she indicated the right of the picture. "The car you can see here is Joe's. Both Sheila and Brenda have assured me of that, and you can see it's the correct colour. From the shape of the bit of the roof you can see, I'm sure your experts will confirm it's a Ford Ka." Digging back into the briefcase, she came out with a ruler and laid it so it was level with the roof of the car, intersecting Joe's image just below shoulder level. "Compare Joe's height to that of the car. I told you, I've met with him a few times, and I reckon he's about five feet five at best."

"I assume this is leading somewhere?" Dockerty asked. "Rather than simply commenting on how short he is."

Denise dug into her case again, and came out with her processed stills from the building security cameras, and selected one showing the grainy image of a dark-clothed man standing alongside Joe's car, having just got out.

"Where did you get that?" Dockerty demanded.

"If you must know, I bribed the security officer for a copy of the recording." She chuckled. "I told you. The insurance companies are not interested in PACE."

"Security were advised they couldn't share that footage with anyone. It's evidence in a potential crown prosecution, for God's sake."

"Yes, I know, but they're not stupid." Denise smiled slyly. "When I told them it could prove Joe innocent and they might be facing a lawsuit, they were only too happy to help." Now she laughed. "Mind you, the twenty quid I dropped Todd Henshaw might have tripped the final switch." More soberly, she went on. "Forget where I got it from, Ray, and check this out." Again she placed the ruler so that it was in line with the car roof. This time it intersected the figure at chest height. "The angle is difficult, and the picture isn't good, but this man is obviously a good deal taller than Joe." Leaving everything as it was on Dockerty's desk, she sat back. "You've got the wrong man,

Ray."

For a long time, Dockerty sat, staring silently at the two images. At length, he picked up the ruler, and carried out the same checks as Denise had done.

"I need our people to look into this."

"Come on, Ray. It's not Joe. Or do you think he was wearing ridiculous high heels like those Elton John wore as the Pinball Wizard in *Tommy*?"

"It doesn't clear Murray."

"It casts doubt on your case against him. And when you finally admit that, he's gonna kick your arse from here to hell and back."

Dockerty snatched up the phone and dialled. "Get me a photo genius in here. Now." While he waited, he concentrated on Denise. "I'm not saying it's Murray, I'm not saying it's not Murray, but even if it isn't him, how do we know Murray didn't pay this man to do this?"

"You got any evidence for that?"

"No."

"So you'd still have to free Joe."

There was a polite knock on the door and a young officer entered. Dockerty handed him the CCTV image. "Check on the height of a Ford Ka, and then estimate the height of this man. Phone the results through to me the minute you have them. And I want them in ten minutes."

"Yes, sir."

The officer left and closed the door behind him. Dockerty gazed sternly at Denise. "You are making life difficult for me... just like you did when you were a cop."

"Yes, and I was right more than wrong then, too, wasn't I? Come off it, Ray. You may be hard, but you're straight. As long as I've known you, you've never liked seeing an innocent man walled up. You've never gone for the quick kill. You never decided a man was guilty and then looked for evidence to fit the charge. You looked for the evidence first."

"And if Joe is innocent, I'll free him."

Half an hour later, Dockerty sat with Chief Superintendent Oughton, who looked grimly from the photograph to his subordinate.

"There's no doubt, Ray?"

"None," Dockerty admitted. "Joe Murray is about five feet four, five feet five at best. Our preliminary estimate is that the man in this picture is about six feet six inches tall. It's not Murray."

As Dockerty had done previously, Oughton picked up both photographs and studied them. At length he put down the one of Joe and tapped the other as he spoke.

"Does this clear Joe from our investigation?"

"Nothing of the kind. There are too many questions left open for me to drop him." Dockerty sighed. "But if I'd had this a few days ago, I wouldn't have been so quick to haul him into court. Not because I'm sure of his innocence. To be perfectly frank, Don, I've always been doubtful. But this would have let me give him the benefit of that doubt."

Oughton cleared his throat purposely. "Remind me. Why didn't we ask for bail when he appeared in court?"

"You know the score as well as I do. It's a murder charge. At the time, we were sufficiently certain of ourselves to ask for him to be remanded on suspicion. It's not practice to release suspected killers on bail, and as I said in court, his ex-wife lives in the Canary Islands. But I also said it was no more than a minor worry. I didn't suggest that Joe would jump on the next plane to Tenerife, and I didn't specifically oppose bail. It was the magistrate's decision and I wasn't going to argue with it."

Oughton shrugged. "What do you want me to do?"

"I know it's Saturday, Don, but we need to move quickly on this before things deteriorate beyond our control. If you can get a magistrate and ask him to release Joe into our custody, I'll apologise to Gemma for the rough ride I've given her, and send her along to the court to deal with it. Once I have Joe back here, I'll free him on police bail."

"A couple of points, Ray. Why didn't we ask for extended custody here at the station?"

"First, I had almost enough evidence to charge him. Second, once again, it's not best practice to keep a prisoner here, where we're short on manpower, and when we're this close to a charge." Dockerty held up his hand, thumb and forefinger millimetres apart. "And I did tell you this before I took him to court."

"All right. Next question, why send Gemma to ask for his release? Why not go yourself?"

"Because I'm going out to Sanford nick to collect him."

Oughton's eyes widened. "You know what will happen? You know how Joe will react."

Dockerty nodded. "It's my responsibility. I'm leading the case. If he's going to scream at anyone, he can scream at me. I can deal with it."

"And when he's through screaming?"

Dockerty smiled. "Then I start to use that fine mind of his."

"Ray—"

Dockerty interrupted again. "I said, didn't I, that I had my doubts. I've run this by the book, Don, but it's one of these where the book isn't necessarily the best way. We both know Joe. His powers of observation aren't just a legend, they're a fact. If Denise Latham spotted something as tiny as this—" Dockerty waved his hand at the CCTV image "— what is Joe likely to spot? And you know as well as I, that he'll be more than eager to shove his nose in. Anything to rub our faces in it. No, Don, now that we know this, the best place for Joe Murray is not kicking his heels in the nick, but out here pushing for the truth."

Oughton gathered the evidence together and slipped it back into the folder, before handing it over to his subordinate. "Rather you than me. I'll get onto the courts and see if they can find a magistrate. You carry on and brief Gemma."

With a brisk nod, Dockerty got to his feet and left.

Joe stepped out of HM Prison Sanford at just after twelve noon. He had learned half an hour earlier that he was to be freed and that someone would collect him outside the prison.

He would find it hard to describe the relief he felt when given the news. While having been given permission to stay in the prison library for most of the time, he had still passed another two nights in the company of the garrulous Eric Neave, and by Friday evening, his cellmate was getting on his nerves so much that he really felt like strangling the old man.

"I admit we didn't get on too well, me and Annie, but she reckoned it were cos I spent too much time on me allotment looking after me azalea bush. I mighta bin fed up of the old sow, but I didn't hate her enough to kill her."

Joe felt his nerves beginning to fray, and matters got worse when Neave's voice came out of the darkness, asking, "How about you, then? You hate the woman you murdered, did you?"

"It was man, not a woman, and yes I did hate him, but I didn't kill him." With that, Joe tried to sleep again.

"So what had he done to make you hate him? Criticise your garden, did he?"

"He burned down my business," Joe said, and shut his eyes again. He also closed his mind to Neave's rambling.

Sheila and Brenda had visited again on Friday, telling him Denise was onto something.

"We don't know what," Sheila said. "She hasn't told us. But she thinks it might prove you innocent."

"Prove me innocent, or just cast doubt on my guilt?" Joe demanded.

Brenda had replied with a weak smile. "We're not sure."

They passed the remainder of the hour chattering, telling him how much support he had in the community, how everyone was looking forward to seeing his name cleared and having him back behind the counter of his café, where he belonged.

When they left, Joe spent another two hours in the library, following up one of his theories, his mind worrying on the inconclusive snippets his two companions had delivered. He would believe in Denise Latham when she actually had something concrete and constructive to say.

At eleven thirty on Saturday morning, Harvey Thornton told him his release was imminent, and Joe revised his opinion of Denise.

Over the past six months, she had called into the café on a number of occasions, and were it not for the fact that she was trying to prove him guilty of burning down his old café, he would have found her quite attractive. Even through her business-like manner, she exuded the air of a fun-loving, single woman; easy and pleasant company.

Packing away his few belongings, ready to return to the real world, he thought perhaps it was time to build a few bridges with her.

Coming out of the prison into the hot outside world, clutching his personal effects under his arm, screwing up his eyes in the strong sunlight, he scanned the car park and there were only a few cars on it, one of which he recognised immediately.

"I'm your ride back to town, Joe," Dockerty said, climbing out of the car.

"Then I'll walk." Joe made as if to spit at the ground. "If I never see you again, Dockerty, other than swinging on the end of a rope, it'll be too soon."

Dockerty opened the passenger door. "Get in the car, Joe."

"Are you deaf or just plain stupid? Thinking about it, I suppose the way you threw me in jail should tell me all I need to know."

"Either get in the car or I'll arrest you again."

Joe's temper began to get the better of him. "What the hell are you talking about? I've just been freed."

"No. You've been released into the custody of the Sanford police. When we get back to the station, I will release you on police bail. Between now and then, we have a lot to talk about and obviously you have a lot to get off your chest. Well, I'm not willing to stand in the middle of an open car park, providing spectator sport for anyone who might be watching. For the last time, get in the car or I'll cuff you and force you in."

Furious, impotent, left without leeway, Joe did as bidden and settled into the passenger seat of Dockerty's Volvo.

Dockerty came back around the car and climbed into the driver's seat. Closing the door, he started the engine and turned up the air-conditioning.

As the superintendent pulled out of the car and picked up the signs for Sanford, Joe tore into him.

"You threw me in there without so much as a by your leave. Four days I've been in that hellhole. Four bloody days locked up with some nutjob rabbiting on about his bleeding azalea bush."

"Eric Neave," Dockerty said. "Murdered his wife. We know he did it, but we can't find the final piece of the puzzle."

"Forget Neave. Think about Joe Murray and what you've done to him. I will sue you and your department for every penny I can get. I will bankrupt you. By the time I've finished, none of you will get a job guarding the sweet stall in a supermarket."

"There are rules, Joe, and I have to play by them. The evidence I had compelled me to go to court. It was their decision to remand you."

"Only because you said you were close to charging me."

"The only alternative was Sanford police station, and we were so short of bodies it wasn't an alternative. I had no choice."

"So what's happened now? Has Don Oughton agreed to the overtime so I can be held there?"

"No. Fresh evidence has turned up which has cast doubt on the case against you."

The announcement caught Joe unawares and brought him up short. "Fresh evidence? What evidence?"

They were on the outskirts of town, pushing in towards the centre, the early Saturday afternoon traffic clogging the roads and holding them back.

Held up at the busy junction of Selby Road and Pontefract Road, waiting in a queue to turn right, Dockerty took advantage of the hiatus to detail first the extraneous drum of cooking oil, and then the figure on the CCTV image. It took two more changes of the lights before they finally turned the corner, by which time Joe had been brought up to date.

The information did nothing to calm Joe's anger. "I told you all along someone was trying to frame me, didn't I? But you didn't want to listen, did you? Oh, no. You just waded in, size thirteen boots trampling over everything and everyone. You had your suspect and that was good enough for you."

Dockerty remained remarkably calm under Joe's verbal assault. "I did my job. The evidence against you was too strong. And to be honest, Joe, you're not out of it yet."

"What? After all the evidence you've just told me, you still believe I'm guilty? You're an idiot, managing a team of idiots."

Dockerty gritted his teeth as they arrived on the inner ring road, its two lanes packed with slow moving traffic. "All I know for certain, Joe, is that you did not drop that extra drum in your lockup. But how do I know you didn't pay someone to do it?"

"I don't know anyone who's six and a half feet tall."

"Yes you do."

"Name one person."

Dockerty did not even have to think about it. "Your nephew, Lee. It was his knife we found at Vaughan's place. He's well over six feet tall, and he does as you tell him. And if you're not involved have you ever considered that it might be him trying to frame you?"

Joe shook his head. "Lee doesn't have the brains to put together something as complicated as this. It takes him all his time to work out how to fasten his bootlaces."

"His wife then."

"Cheryl's a lovely lass and there is no way she would do this. You're barking up the wrong tree… again. Besides, if Vaughan was murdered in his living room, how would Lee get in there? It's not like they were—"

Making the turn into Gale Street, Dockerty cut Joe off. "Have you ever wondered about the fire at the original Lazy Luncheonette?"

"I wonder about it all the time. Like I told the insurance investigator, I grew up in that building and I lived there all my life."

"The accelerant was cooking oil."

"That same setup as was used at Vaughan's place. I know."

Dockerty turned into the police yard, pausing at the barrier to announce himself to the control clerk in the building. Driving through, reversing into a spot near the back entrance, he cut the engine, released his seatbelt, and half turned to face Joe.

"You and your friends were in Blackpool at the time. So was Vaughan. So it was obvious that neither of you could have started the fire. But suppose Vaughan had persuaded your nephew to do it."

"Then Vaughan was a bigger idiot than I took him for," Joe retorted. "I have to watch Lee when he's lighting the gas burners so he doesn't set fire to himself. And tell me what Lee would gain from all this? Burning down the old place and then framing me for Vaughan's murder."

"Who gets the café if you're out of the picture?"

"Lee gets eighty per cent of it. Sheila and Brenda get the other twenty per cent. I've told you once, Dockerty, you're looking at the wrong man."

The superintendent opened his door, ready to get out. "Nevertheless, when we're done here, I'm taking you back to The Lazy Luncheonette and I'll want a word with Lee."

Joe checked his watch. "Well, you'd better hurry up. It's Saturday and they all knock off at two."

They got out of the car and Joe hurried alongside

Dockerty into the building, rushing to keep up with the taller man's longer stride.

"By the way, how did you twig the difference in height? Gemma or Ike?"

"Neither. An old friend of yours. Mine too, as it happens. Denise Latham."

Joe was satisfied. "She spent months accusing me of torching the old place and I had my doubts when Sheila and Brenda told me she was on the case, but they also told me she was onto something. Good to know she saw sense. It's one I owe her."

"You may have to do more than you think, Joe." Dockerty grinned. "I think she fancies you."

Joe gawped.

Chapter Eleven

Lee and the women were getting ready to shut down and go home when Joe and Dockerty finally arrived at The Lazy Luncheonette.

Mid-afternoon on a Saturday had never been the busiest of times, but the café had only reopened that morning, and things were worse than usual. Just one customer sat at a window table with the remnants of an apple pie and a cup of tea in front of her. Denise sat off to one side, Sheila, Brenda and Lee were busy with as much of the cleaning as they could manage, while keeping an eye on their only customer, ready to lock up the moment she left.

After the effusive greetings were over and done with, or in Denise's case, a smile and a handshake, Dockerty took Joe and Lee to one side. Joe had insisted on being present when Dockerty questioned his nephew.

"I'm not trying to railroad him," Dockerty protested, noticing that the three women had taken the table across the aisle where they could comfortably listen in.

"I know you're not, but Lee's a gormless sod at the best of times. One leading question and you'll nail him for the fire at the Crystal Palace, and that happened twenty years before I was born, never mind him. Besides, I have ways of making him tell the absolute truth."

When challenged, Lee was amiability personified. "You think I mighta killed him?" He laughed gregariously. "Will I get me name in the papers?"

"Guaranteed," Joe said. "Stop fooling around, Lee. Where were you between half ten and half eleven on Monday night. And I want the truth."

Lee blushed. "I were at home in bed with our Cheryl. We

were..." His cheeks flushed redder. "You know."

Joe clucked. "I said I want the truth, not the gory details."

"There's only you and your wife who could confirm that?" Dockerty asked.

His face still glowing, Lee looked uncomfortable. "Well, I dunno. Our Cheryl don't like to talk about it. It's private innit?"

Joe fumed again. "The superintendent means is there anyone other than Cheryl who can confirm you were at home, not what you were doing to her."

"I weren't doing anything to her. She were doing it to me."

Joe looked down, held a hand to his forehead and shook his head. "Saints preserve me from sex-obsessed idiots." He looked again at Lee, and with enforced patience asked, "Can anyone else tell us you were at home all night on Monday?"

After a moment's thought, Lee offered, "Our Danny."

"The word of a child won't cut much ice, Lee," Dockerty said. "Let's move on from there, eh? Can you remember before the old Lazy Luncheonette burned down, did Gerard Vaughan ever approach you and ask you to persuade your Uncle Joe to sell?"

"Oh him, yeah. He collared me in the Foundry Inn one afternoon after I'd finished work. I told him to bugger off. Then later, he turned up here again and asked again. Said he needed to get The Lazy Luncheonette demolished. I told him where he could go. He had these two bruisers with him." Lee grinned. "I did me Clint Eastwood impression, Uncle Joe. I said to him, 'go ahead, skunk, make my day'."

Joe felt steam coming from his ears. "Punk, not skunk."

Lee chuckled. "Whatever. I'd have ripped him and his mates to bits."

The younger man's amiability did little to quell Joe's frustration. "How come you never told me about this?"

"Well, you had a lot on your mind at the time, and I didn't wanna bother you by getting into fights. I told Aunty Brenda and Aunty Sheila."

Joe glanced across at the two women.

"He did," Brenda said.

"And we didn't want to bother you either, Joe," Sheila confirmed.

Determined to stick to the point, Dockerty asked, "Did Vaughan suggest you might make a lot of money by burning the place down?"

Lee's eyes widened. "Crikey, no. I'd have had to tell Uncle Joe about that. It's illegal, innit? Arsing?"

"Arson," Joe snapped. "The only arsing around here is you arsing about."

"Did your Uncle Joe ask you to bring his car here on Monday night, and drop off a drum of cooking oil in the storage cupboard?" Dockerty demanded.

"No. I didn't know Uncle Joe wanted a drum dropping off in the storage cupboard," Lee replied.

Joe sighed. "As a defence witness, the prosecution would love him. Dockerty, you're chasing your tail, here. Monday night had nothing to do with me, Lee or Sheila and Brenda. Or at least if it was Sheila and Brenda, Sheila would have to sit on Brenda's shoulders."

"Charming," Sheila commented from across the room. "Superintendent, Joe is right. Neither I, nor Brenda, nor Lee would do anything to jeopardise this business, and Joe is not only our employer, but our friend, too."

Dockerty watched as the only customer left the café, and then spoke. "Mrs Riley, right now I'm trying to clear both Joe and Lee from this investigation." He glanced at Lee. "I don't believe Lee is involved, but I do have to question him. And whether or not I believe Joe to be innocent, I still have too much evidence pointing at him."

Having listened without comment, Denise spoke up. "Lee, what size shoe do you take?"

"Fourteen. I can take a thirteen at a pinch." He laughed. "But they do pinch." He laughed again. "D'yer gerrit, Uncle Joe?"

"Yeah, yeah, I get it. Remind me the next time you're on telly. I'll make sure I'm out." He addressed Dockerty.

"What would Lee's shoe size have to do with anything?"

"Forensic picked up a latent print in the footwell of your car. They estimate a size eleven to twelve." Dockerty turned a sour eye on Denise. "And I wish I'd never mentioned it to you."

The news only fuelled Joe's irritation. "That should have told you it wasn't me."

"Nothing of the kind. Lee may not be able to squeeze into a size twelve, but you could. It's only when we take that print and the height of the driver as determined by Denise, that we can say it was neither you nor Lee. But, Joe, that doesn't mean you couldn't have paid someone to set all this up." Dockerty held up his hands to stem the howl of protest. "All right, all right. I know it's not likely, but while the possibly is there, I have to consider it, and I'm sorry, but I can't scratch you from my list of suspects."

"And how long is that list?" Joe demanded.

"Yours is the only name on it." Again Dockerty hastened on. "However, Gemma and Ike Barrett will be getting to it first thing Monday morning."

Joe tutted. "People keep saying they don't believe I did this, and yet when you ask, mine is the only name that comes up. Well, I'm not gonna sit here and wait for you and our Gemma to clear my name."

"Hear, hear," said Denise. "And I'm with you, Joe. I've a lot of money riding on this."

Dockerty greeted the announcements with implacable calm. "I didn't expect anything else, but I have to say, you're not dealing with some domestic, here, Joe, Denise. Cutting Joe out of the equation presents us with the profile of a man who's very clever."

"How do you know it's a man?" Joe demanded.

"Fire is a man's weapon," the superintendent replied. "And I don't know many women who wear a size twelve shoe… but that could be a blind. We've found very little in the way of forensics, and none of it hints at a woman, so until we can demonstrate otherwise, we work on the assumption that it's a man. And a dangerous man at that.

130

I'm telling you because I know you won't sit back, but if you get close to this man, he won't hesitate to get rid of you."

"Where do you get that from, Ray?" Denise asked.

"Vaughan's killing. We have no clear motive for it, so it's safe to say it was something between them. Everything does point at precise planning. The way it was blamed on you, Joe, the way everything was set up to make you appear guilty. Even down to getting into the recycling shed and making sure he was caught on CCTV. He is careful, and we have no direction, yet. If you two get close, he will not hesitate to guard himself. He will kill the pair of you. If you come across anything, anything at all, please bring it to me. I get paid to take risks when dealing with killers. All you'll get is a line in the obituary columns." Dockerty stood. "You probably have a little celebrating to do, so I'll leave you to it." With a brisk nod at each of them in turn, he left.

Sheila ushered him through the door with muted thanks, and locked it behind him. Coming back to her seat, she asked, "Can we call it a day, Joe? Brenda and I have a party to arrange at the Miner's Arms."

"Someone's birthday?" Joe asked with a wink.

"You know full well it's in your honour." Brenda beamed on Denise. "And you're invited too."

"Wouldn't miss it."

"You might," Joe advised, and turned his attention to his crew. "Is there much cleaning to do?"

"Only these few cups." Brenda indicated the beakers from which they had all been drinking.

"I'll see to them. Get yourselves home. Denise, could you hang back? I'd like a word."

"No problem."

"And I'll catch you lot at the Miner's Arms tonight, but we may be a little late."

"As long as you're there," Brenda said as she made for the door behind Sheila and Lee.

Joe let them out, locked up behind them and rejoined Denise.

"I owe you," he said.

"And North Shires owe me a fortune, Joe. Or they will do by the time I'm through with this."

"I don't care about them. I care that you got me out of the nick. After all the months you spent hassling me, you still pulled out the stops when it mattered. I want to say thanks, properly. Have dinner with me tonight."

Her face broke into a broad, beaming smile, and her eyes lit up. Suspicion set in almost as quickly. "Not here, I hope?"

"Hell no. What do you take me for?"

"A tightwad. At least that's what Sheila and Brenda told me."

"Remind me to have a word with them. No, listen, I know the maître d' at Churchill's I'm sure I can get us a table. You know where it is?"

"Just off the motorway as you come into Sanford."

"That's the one. How about it?"

She checked her watch. "I'll have to go home and change. Say half past seven?"

"That'll do fine. We can have a bit of a feed, then push onto the Miner's Arms if you're game."

"Oh, I've always been game, Joe. I just hope we're talking about the same game."

***

The Ronaldo Lombardy Combo, a quartet composed of trombone, guitar, keyboard and drums, were a semi-permanent fixture at Churchill's. They were working their way through Horst Jankowski's *Walk in the Black Forest* as Joe and Denise took delivery of their main course.

Joe wore his best suit, complete with crisp white shirt and black bow tie, while Denise had settled for a dark, knee-length dress which hung a little loosely on her, an acceptable cross between formal and casual evening wear.

With typical lack of originality, Joe chose fillet steak, and Denise opted for a mixed grill. He noticed that she ate with

132

gusto, as if this were the first meal she had enjoyed in a long time. He picked and nibbled at his meal. After prison food, it really was the first decent meal he had had in several days, and he was wary of upsetting his volatile stomach.

Throughout the starter course, they kept the conversation neutral; the recent hot weather, Wimbledon, holidays already behind them, or up and coming. But as they completed their main meal, and worked their way slowly through a dessert of strawberry trifle, Joe gradually brought up the subject of the work she had done on his behalf.

"There's no big secret, Joe, and no hidden agenda."

"It's to do with the fire at the original Lazy Luncheonette."

"Yes." Denise sipped a mouthful of house white. "Who burned the place down?"

"Gerard Vaughan. Not personally. He can't have done. We know exactly where he was when it started… or at least, we think we do. Blackpool is only an hour and a half away."

"He was definitely in Blackpool. His hotel confirmed it, and when I checked their CCTV recordings, he never left the place. The police, naturally, had already made those checks." She smiled. "For reference, they'd already checked you, too, and we know you were nowhere near Sanford when the place was torched."

"All of which means Vaughan paid someone to set it. But I don't see—"

"Correct," she cut in. "That was my belief all along. Obviously I had to investigate you. There was that outside chance you were making mischief. But I never really believed it."

"You showed up at the café often enough."

Denise's smile was coquettish this time. "We'll talk about that later. For now, let's accept that Vaughan paid someone to do the job. The Fire Service report said it was amateur. A couple of bricks knocked out from the party wall to the minimarket next door, petrol, cooking oil and a candle to set it off. But suppose our torch wanted us to think he was an amateur? Suppose he was a real professional who decided to make it look like an amateur job? How much would he cost Vaughan?"

"Thousands, I suppose. But what does this have to do with Vaughan's murder?"

"Plenty, if you'll give me time to get there."

She took another sip of her wine as Ronaldo and his combo struck up *Fly Me to the Moon*.

Raising her voice a little so she could be heard over the music, she went on, "Such arrangements are a two-way street. Vaughan could never go to the police and hand over the torch because he would go to prison for instigating the crime. And the torch could never go to the cops about Vaughan for precisely the same reason."

"A Mexican standoff."

"Correct. And there's only one way out of it."

The light came on in Joe's brain. "One kills the other."

"Correct again, give that man prize."

Denise laughed, and spent a few moments watching one or two couples who had taken to the dance floor.

"Tempting," she said, "and I bet you're mean mover."

"I can go some, if you want."

"I'll pass if you don't mind, Joe. I haven't had enough to drink yet."

Joe laughed. "You need to be drunk to dance?"

"Not drunk. Just light-headed enough to lose a few inhibitions. Don't you?"

He shook his head. "Nope. My old ma taught me how to dance when I was a kid. Waltz, foxtrot, quickstep, even the cha-cha-cha and jive." He laughed again. "Can't say I remember them all, but I do remember how boring life was back then with the old man and our Arthur working the café, and me and Ma upstairs with nothing better to do."

Denise shook her head in admiration. "You're full of surprises, Joe. I'll bet she didn't teach you an Argentinean tango."

"Too naughty. So go on. Your theory on the killing. Did it just come to you right out of nowhere?"

She toyed with her glass as she answered. "No. It came

from Ray Dockerty, although he doesn't know it because he's not interested in the original fire."

Joe's eyebrows rose. "I'm all ears."

Denise was quiet for a moment, as if she was formulating her words. "I think the man who murdered Vaughan is the same one who torched your old place. And he did it because he wanted out from the hold Vaughan had over him."

Joe whistled inaudibly over the noise of Ronaldo and his pals running into Gershwin's *Rhapsody in Blue*.

"You don't believe me?" Denise asked.

"It's a possibility, but there are others. Tell me where it came from."

"The hard drive was missing from Vaughan's laptop. After I showed Ray that it couldn't have been you getting out of that car on Monday night, he went through the whole case with me, and the moment he mentioned the missing hard drive, I understood. Where would a man like Vaughan keep evidence against an arsonist he had employed? On his laptop. Probably locked up with a really strong password. Difficult to break into, but if Vaughan is already dead, it's simpler to spend a bit of time removing the hard drive."

"It would have been even simpler to take the laptop away with him."

"Not if he wanted to pin it on you, Joe," Denise argued.

"Good point," he agreed.

"You said there are alternative theories?"

"One or two, but I think we've talked enough shop for tonight, don't you?" He checked his watch. "It's getting on for nine, what say I settle the bill and we move to the Miner's Arms?"

"You'll have to show your face, I suppose." Denise made it sound as if it was the last thing she wanted him to do.

"The party is in my honour." He stood up, collected her cardigan, and helped her into it. "What the hell do you want with a woolly on a night like tonight?"

"Purely for show."

After a brief delay while Joe settled the bill, they stepped out into the hot night and Denise promptly removed her

135

cardigan. Because his car was still with the police, he had arrived by taxi. Now they climbed into her car for the short journey to the pub.

Slotting the key into the ignition, she started the engine, and faced Joe. "If I have even one more drink, I won't be able to drive home."

"I'm sure we'll find somewhere for you to sleep."

"At your place?"

Joe blushed. "Well er, sure. Why not? It's small, but cosy you know. And I can always doss on the settee for the night."

Denise smiled tipsily, and tossed her cardigan over her shoulder onto the back seat. "Oh no. I may need something to keep me warm in the night."

And Joe blushed again.

Chapter Twelve

The sun blazed onto the front approach to Queen's Court when Joe sat in the widow of his third floor flat the following morning. He was not entirely at peace with the world, but he was a good deal more cheerful than he had been for the last few days.

And a part of that increased optimism stepped into the living room wearing one of his shirts to protect her modesty.

"Can't remember when I've had such a good time," Denise said, joining him at the table.

"Just goes to show you. Keep your Leeds. You wanna good night out, dine at Churchill's then come and join the fun at the Miner's Arms with the Sanford 3rd Age Club."

"I think it could be a good night in with Joe Murray, too."

Her words recalled the passion of the previous night. Joe deliberately suppressed it.

"So," Denise went on, "it looks like we have a lot of work in front of us if we're gonna clear your name."

"We?" Joe raised his eyebrows inviting elucidation.

"You don't think I'm going to cut and run now, do you? I have a lot of money invested in the fire at your old place."

Joe sipped his tea. "You still think the two events, the fire and Vaughan's murder, are linked?"

"You don't?"

Joe shook his head and put down his beaker. "Only in passing. They may be linked, I don't know, but it doesn't necessarily follow."

Now Denise raised her eyebrows, and Joe clasped his beaker in both hands.

"You investigated Vaughan as well as me. You must know what kind of man he was."

137

"Very smooth," Denise replied. "Suave, sophisticated, upright pillar of the community, and an honest businessman to look at his public profile."

"And given to dirty tricks to get what he wants."

"Okay. I'll go with that. You said you had alternatives."

"I did. Let's imagine for one minute that his death has nothing to do with the old Lazy Luncheonette. He had plenty of projects all over Yorkshire, so let's imagine it was to do with something else. That street he lived on, for example. Eastward. The old Sanford Main Pit was located in the south of the town, but for the sake of argument, let's say one of the galleries ran in the general direction of Eastward. Now, I don't care how good your foundations are, there will be some subsidence. The pit bottom was between five and six hundred yards below ground, but even so, there will still be some slip in it. To take this argument further, let's imagine one of the other residents on Eastward complained to Vaughan about cracks in the walls, sink holes in the gardens, and so on. And let's further imagine that Vaughan gave them the bum's rush." Joe put on a false, classless accent. "'Yes, yes, Mr X, I'll get it seen to'." He reverted to his normal, Yorkshire, tones. "Eventually, Mr X gets fed up and decides he's gonna bump off Vaughan. The fire at the old Lazy Luncheonette was big news in this town. I still have the cuttings somewhere. My arguments with Vaughan and the way Ballantynes' took him over were just as big. I made sure of that. So Mr X decides he's gonna make me the patsy. He murders Vaughan and torches the house in the same way as The Lazy Luncheonette, and points the finger at me."

"Interesting idea," Denise agreed after giving it some thought. "But which development, and who?"

Joe left the table, crossed to a display unit, and took out an envelope folder. Bringing it back, he removed several documents, one of which was a technical drawing detailing the galleries of the old Sanford Main Colliery, and beneath it was a town plan.

Placing the technical plan on the map, he pressed hard

down on it so the map could be seen through the thin upper sheet.

"I wasn't entirely idle in the nick, and Harvey Thornton let me photocopy the plan of the mine workings. I'm lining this up as well as I can," he said, "but look where the Aire Gallery runs."

The gallery was one of four marked on the plan, and it ran slightly northeast, and beneath it, they could just make out the sweeping drive of Eastward.

"Clever," Denise agreed. "Now all we need is the who... and, obviously we need the answers to some pretty searching questions. Like, how did he get hold the knife and pen? How did he get hold of your car keys? How did he get hold of the two keys for the outside glory hole? Is he six feet four?"

"It doesn't matter who we look at, or how we think he did it, all those questions need answering. And the car key is easy to answer. We lost one a few weeks ago. At least we thought we did. Only it wasn't lost. It was nicked."

"Who could have taken it?"

"Fire, police, workmen, even Vaughan. I don't know."

"Which means you can't answer the questions you've just posed."

"Neither can Dockerty, which is why I'm still top of his hit parade. Come on, Denise, if you're helping here, you're help... Hang on a minute. How much is this going to cost me?"

She smiled. "Nothing. I told you, I'm hoping it'll lead me to the torch who burned down The Lazy Luncheonette."

"And if it doesn't?"

"Then you can owe me, and I'll take payment in kind."

Joe sniggered. "If you're sure. Now, let's think about the pen and the knife. How did they get from the ruin of the old café to Vaughan's house. Plenty of options. Vaughan himself could have taken them as a souvenir, and his killer found them and used them. There are others who could have taken them, too. The demolition crew, the firemen, cops, council-employed health and safety wallahs who were round the place that morning. Mr X could have bought them off someone when he planned to incriminate me."

"And your car?" Denise demanded. "What we saw on the CCTV could well have been a ringer, Joe. A stolen car with your plate put on," she went on obviously uncertain whether Joe understood the term 'ringer'. "But the fact remains he did get into your car to leave the mark of the drum and the trace of oil in the boot. He would need a key for that."

"Would he?" Joe asked. "What I know about breaking into cars is zip. But I do know that my car has only an immobiliser fitted. No alarm. You need a chipped key to start the engine, but do you need it to open the boot?"

"He would still need a key that fitted. When I inquired, only one key cutter owned up to cutting *and chipping* a key for a Ford Ka. And he remembered the customer… you."

"So, it could have been a ringer, as you put it, and he could have had a key which fitted my boot. See, Denise, as far as I'm concerned, my car never left the car park here on Monday night. I parked it at the end of the building on Monday and it was still there Tuesday. It never moved. I know these are tough questions, but we have to ask them."

"It's Sunday. We won't get much done today, but tell me where you want to start."

"On Eastward."

"Why there?"

"Because it seems to me a huge coincidence that this witness, this Rodney Spencer sort, spotted a car like mine on Monday night. What was he doing out there before the fire started?"

Denise chuckled. "A disgruntled house buyer?"

"Right."

She laughed again. "Okay. If I can take a shower, let's get out there."

"There is a problem. I have no car. The cops still have it."

"No problem. We can use mine. I'll bill the insurance company for the mileage."

He tutted. "If I tried to fiddle my insurance company like that, I'd have you all over me."

Denise paused in the doorway and looked over her shoulder. "After last night, Joe, you can have me all over you anytime you want."

***

Rodney Spencer was as angry to be disturbed by Joe and Denise as he had been when the police dragged him out of bed on Tuesday morning, and Joe took an instant dislike to him.

In his mid-fifties, if Joe was any judge, he was short and rotund, his distended midriff aggravated by a light grey T-shirt with narrow, red, horizontal stripes, and a bagging pair of jogging pants. Beneath his thinning head of curly, grey hair, a pair of dark framed glasses were perched indignantly upon his bulbous nose.

When they explained why they were calling, he did not invite them into his spacious bungalow, but harangued them on the doorstep.

"I told the police all I know, now go away."

"You told them you'd seen my car at Vaughan's house," Joe retaliated.

"No. I told them I had seen a Ford Ka. If they choose to imagine it's yours, that's their affair and you should discuss it with them. Now—"

"So what were you doing wandering the streets at eleven o'clock Monday night?" Joe interrupted.

"I think that's my business," Spencer snapped.

"Not if it turns out you torched Vaughan's place and tried to blame it on me."

Spencer's outrage increased. "I happen to be the investment manager for the Leeds branch of a national bank. I don't murder people."

"No, you just rob them blind with management charges."

"How dare you?"

Having stood by watching with amusement, Denise now stepped into the argument in an effort to quell it. "Would that be the Westmoreland and North Riding Bank, Mr

141

Spencer?"

"Yes. What of it?"

"They're partnered with North Shires Insurance." Denise aimed a thumb at Joe. "He's insured with that company, and I do a lot of work for them."

"Do you indeed?"

She sighed. "Mr Spencer, you'll forgive me, but if you deal with your customer queries like this, you'd be hauled over the coals. Now, I'm investigating both the fire at Mr Murray's old premises, and the fire at Mr Vaughan's. Mr Murray has been cleared of any involvement… almost, and we're keen to help the police in any way we can. I'm sure Mr Murray didn't mean to accuse you of the crime, but it would help if you could tell us how you came to see this Ford turn up at Vaughan's place?"

"I was walking my dog, if you must know. He's getting on in years, and I always walk him late at night to ensure there are no, er, accidents, if you take my meaning. Now if that's all…"

Spencer left the idea hanging, hinting that they should go away.

"Not quite," Denise said. "May I ask, did you or any of your neighbours have, er, problems with Vaughan? You know, house subsiding or anything like that?"

"I can't speak for my neighbours, but for myself, from a business point of view, I never found Gerard Vaughan anything but professional. We knew before we bought the house that it was built over old mine workings, and such minor problems as we did have with subsidence, were put right quickly and with the minimum of fuss. He was, as I say, thoroughly professional."

"He was a crook who burned my café down," Joe argued.

Spencer looked over his glasses and down his nose. "That is matter for the police, I should imagine."

Denise spoke before Joe could cause more argument. "That was the businessman. What about personally."

Again Spencer's look was one of undisguised disdain. "I didn't mix with his sort."

Joe, who had been mentally grumbling at the lauded opinion of Vaughan, looked up sharply. "His sort?"

"Parties up at the big house. Unseemly parties. With plenty of men and women. Not the kind of men and women you would take home to meet your mother. I'm sure you understand me, Mr Murray. Now if you will excuse me, my wife is preparing lunch." Spencer backed into the house, and closed the door behind him.

Joe and Denise gaped at the door, then at each other.

"Does he mean—"

Denise nodded gravely. "They call themselves escorts these days, but it amounts to the same thing."

"Male or female?" Joe asked.

"The way he put it, I thought he meant both."

They turned to walk back to Denise's car, and Joe shook his head. "I knew Vaughan wasn't married, but it doesn't make sense. Why would a man like him with all his millions employ, er, brasses?"

Denise unlocked the car and climbed behind the wheel while Joe settled into the passenger seat. Winding back the sun roof, she said, "Some men do, Joe. They want what they want, but they don't want any involvement. And of course, a hooker is going to do whatever he wants, provided he pays her enough." She paused with her hand on the ignition key. "Where next?"

Joe pursed his lips and stared out at the sun-baked street with its high-priced dwellings. "I'm thinking about it." Turning back so suddenly that he startled her, he said, "This suggests a whole new picture, doesn't it?"

"Does it?"

"How did Vaughan manage to short-circuit so many planning regulations to chuck up his buildings here, there and everywhere?"

"Did he short-circuit them?" Denise asked.

"Put it this way, he didn't meet as much opposition as you might expect. I think that's why he got so mad when I stalled him. He was used to ploughing through council departments in half the time other developers would take, but I held him up."

"So he paid someone to torch the café."

"Do you have any doubts now?"

Denise shook her head. "I haven't had doubts for months, Joe, but I can't prove anything."

"Right, right, right." Joe's irritation showed through. "Let's not get side-tracked again. Let's get back to how he did it, and let's suppose he got some of these people to his parties where they had a grand old time."

"Between the bar and the bed."

"Correct. Then he puts the pressure on. 'Well, Mr Smith, I wouldn't want your wife to learn what you got up to at my place on Saturday night.' 'Well, Mr Jones, are you absolutely certain your employer knows you like to turn the other cheek?' You get my drift?"

"And Mr Smith and Mr Jones toe the line by helping planning applications go through with as little fuss as possible."

"Correct."

"All right. Where and with whom do we follow it up?"

Joe chuckled. "With whom? Bit posh for Sanford on a Sunday afternoon."

Denise smiled by return. "I was brought up to talk proper. Not like you backstreet scruffs."

Joe was not listening. He was still deep in thought, his fingers drumming irritably on his knee.

Snapping out of it, he said, "I have people in mind, but we can't do much about them until tomorrow. But there is one thing we can chase up now."

"Yes?"

"Who had the opportunity to take the pen and the knife from the ruins of the old Lazy Luncheonette? There's one man who might know, and even on Sunday, I know exactly where to find Walt Eshley."

"Who?"

"The demolition contractor." Joe waved at the windscreen. "Drive on. I'll direct you as we go."

Denise mock-saluted. "Very good, sir."

144

***

Walter Eshley was not so much indignant as determined when confronted by Joe and Denise.

"I know what you're trying to say, Joe, but you're knocking on the wrong door. My lads took nowt from that site. They never take anything from any site. They wouldn't dare. It'd be me they were ripping off and I'd cut 'em up for the frying pan if I caught 'em."

In his early sixties, dressed in a shabby suit and an ageing trilby, with an unlit, hand-rolled cigarette dangling from one corner of his mouth, he looked less like a businessman, more like a racecourse tipster, and an unsuccessful one at that. The impression was heightened by a copy of the *Sunday Mirror* jutting from his jacket pocket, but clearly folded with the sports pages open.

His yard was on the industrial side of Sanford, a small, dingy and untidy square of rough land on which were parked several tipper lorries and a low-loader with a large, mechanical digger sat on its trailer.

"We were on standby at Britannia Parade for weeks while you were arguing the toss with the muppets in the town hall. Vaughan was always complaining about the cost of having my crew standing idle. We were supposed to take it down brick by brick, so as not to bother the traffic on Doncaster Road. But, when we finally got the go ahead, on the day of the fire, Brad Kilburn and his pals declared the place unsafe. We had to rip it down with the machine." Eshley waved at the low-loader and its cargo. "If that pen and knife were there, they were buried under the rubble and if anyone found 'em when we'd cleared up. They wouldn't have been in good nick."

"So what are you telling me, Walt?"

"If anyone took 'em on that morning, it had to be either the firemen or plod. They were the only ones who went into the building."

While Denise looked on, Joe strummed his lips. He faced her and raised his eyebrows.

"Could Vaughan have taken them, Mr Eshley?" she asked.

The demolition man shrugged. "Possible, I suppose. I don't remember seeing him go into the site, but he's the kind who'd ride rough over police protests. Kilburn would know. He was the man in charge that day."

Joe and Denise came away no wiser.

"What now?" she asked as they climbed into her car.

"Fire station," he said. "Let's see if we can catch Brad Kilburn."

Denise turned the engine over and pulled on her seatbelt. "How well do you know him?"

"Brad? Known him years. Good, solid, Yorkshire stock. He's a bit younger than me, but he's done well for himself. Took him a couple of tries before he got into the Fire Service, but he's stuck at it. And he's fair, you know. When he checks my place out, he'll find things wrong and tell me to get 'em put right, and as long as I do, he won't report it. Unlike Pemberton and his crowd, Brad cuts you some slack."

"Tough on his crew?"

"As I understand it, he's as tough as he has to be. They have a job to do, he expects everyone to do their job, and if they don't, he kicks. Other than that, he's popular... so I'm told."

The fire station was out of town, on the main Leeds Road, not far from where Joe lived. They found it a hive of inactivity. The three fire engines stood inside their bays, the shutters raised to combat the raw, summer heat. Gleaming, even in the confines of their bays, Joe guessed that the crew had spent the morning polishing and cleaning their vehicles so that they could take it easy during the hottest part of the day.

Red Watch Manager, Fenton Appleton, a year or two younger than Kilburn, greeted them with a warm smile and pleasant handshake, before guiding them to his air-conditioned office and providing soft drinks.

"You're looking for Brad?" Fen sounded surprised. "He's

finished, Joe. Gone. For good."

While Denise took the news with calm equanimity, Joe was surprised. "Finished?"

"Been planning it for months, mate." Fen assured him. "He's put in over twenty-five years and the service was looking to cut senior jobs, so he took the opportunity. Got himself a tidy severance package, and he's landed a plum little job in the Middle East. He's taking that mate of his with him. Corbin."

"They're big pals," Joe explained to Denise. "Brad and Alan Corbin. Some kind of relation, aren't they, Fen?"

"Second cousins eight times removed or summat," Fen agreed. "So what did you want with him?"

As briefly as he could, Joe explained their quest. Fen listened and when Joe had finished, he stroked his chin while staring at the blank wall behind them.

Eventually, he concentrated on them. "I'm not gonna say it doesn't happen. It probably does, although, speaking personally, I've never come across it. But I have to tell you, Joe, if I caught any of my people nicking stuff from fire sites, I'd come down on them like the wrath of God. And I know for a fact Brad would, too. There are rules, y'see. Anything like that could be considered potential forensic evidence and the police might need it, so we don't touch unless we have to and if we do, we report it to the cops and their scientific support people deal with it."

"All right then, Mr Appleton," Denise said, "is it possible Vaughan could have taken those items from the fire at the old Lazy Luncheonette?"

Fen did not answer right away. Instead he looked out through the window onto the rear of the fire station where watch members were sunbathing, one or two of them playing an impromptu game of cricket. When he eventually turned back to face them, his brow was creased.

"I say this, and I shouldn't, but that Vaughan… Do you know what kind of man he was?"

"I've a pretty shrewd idea," Joe replied. "We crossed swords often enough."

"He didn't give that for anyone or anything." Fen snapped his fingers. "The morning the old place burned down, Joe, our boys were all out there. All three tenders, plus crews from Leeds and Wakefield. Brad was technically in charge. It was on his watch. He declared the building unsafe. Police forensic had to go in. So did we. Health and safety bods from the Town Hall went in, against our advice, but they did. Just to satisfy themselves that we were telling it like it was." Fen smiled wanly. "That was your fault, Joe. The stink you kicked up about them demolishing the old parade. They wanted to be sure that the building could not be repaired. That way you couldn't claim that they'd taken advantage of the blaze to get what they wanted."

"I get the picture," Joe assured him.

"Your Gemma had sent Vaughan away with a flea in his ear—"

"I was there," Joe interrupted again.

"But you weren't there when the little snot turned up again at three in the afternoon, were you? Brad had gone home by then, and I was Watch Manager. I warned him, the cops warned him, even Walt Eshley warned him to keep out because it wasn't safe." Fen shook his head. "Didn't take a blind bit of notice. Said that now the place was burned out, it was his, accepted responsibility for his own safety and went in. Now I have to admit, I didn't see him pick anything up, but he was pottering about for a good twenty minutes and I wasn't watching him every minute of the time."

Denise seized on the admission. "So he could have picked up both the pen and the knife."

Fen nodded slowly.

"Yet you didn't report it."

"I reported him entering the site, but Brad was responsible for the final report on that fire and I passed it along to him. He never mentioned it. Probably forgot."

It sounded to Joe as if Fen was on the defensive, and he moved to reassure the fireman. "Administrative box-ticking. The main point is, Vaughan went into that site before it was pulled down. He could have picked up both the knife and the pen." Joe stood up. "Thanks Fen. You've been a great help."

Joe and Denise emerged once more into the heat of Sunday afternoon.

"It proves nothing, Joe," she said as she unlocked the car.

He opened the passenger door and wound down the window before climbing in. "Nothing that any of us, you, me, the cops, have learned, proves anything, but it does open up lines of inquiry. Dockerty hauled me in and locked me up on the strength of the knife and the pen turning up at the fire. But now we know they could have been there all along."

Denise adjusted her seat, ensured the rear-view mirror was right, and slotted the key in the ignition. "Wrong. Ray locked you up on the strength of the video of your car turning up at the rear of The Lazy Luncheonette on the night. He released you the moment I demonstrated that it couldn't have been you." She fired the engine. "On the other hand, you are right about the pen and the knife. They do open up lines of inquiry. If Vaughan had them all along, then his killer knew about it and used them. In fact, I'd go so far as to say they may have prompted him to pin the murder on you."

With the clutch pedal depressed, her hand on the gear lever, she smiled at Joe. "Where next, Sherlock?"

"Don't think there's much more we can do this afternoon. We have other people to see, but they can wait until tomorrow. I'll know where to find them, then."

Chapter Thirteen

Irwin Queenan was predictably outraged when Joe and Denise by-passed his secretary at eleven the following morning. "Get out of here. Now. I don't see anyone without an appointment."

"You'll see us, Irwin," Joe assured him.

Queenan looked past them. "Call security, Miss Darbishire. Have these people removed."

Miss Darbishire made no move to do anything, but simply looked painfully uncomfortably at her boss.

"Alice has more sense, Irwin," Joe said. "She doesn't fancy being charged as an accessory to murder."

The colour rose through Queenan's thick neck to his cheeks, and eventually engulfed his furious face. "How dare you? How bloody dare you accuse me of..." Trailing off he reached for the phone. "I'll call security myself."

"While you're doing that, Mr Queenan, Joe and I will call the police and tell them what we've learned about Vaughan's parties and the people who attended them."

Queenan paused, his finger over the keypad. Looking at each of the three people in turn, he put the receiver down on its cradle and smiled at his secretary. "That will be all for now, Miss Darbishire. I don't want to be disturbed while I'm with Mr Murray and Ms Latham."

"Very good, Mr Queenan."

Joe read Queenan's sudden acquiescence as complete capitulation and he anticipated getting everything he wanted during the next few minutes. He watched Alice Darbishire leave then rounded on Queenan. "I will bury you for this. You and anyone else in this building who was involved in this filth."

"No. It wasn't like that, Joe—"

"You deliberately sold my place out so you could get your jollies with these tarts at Vaughan's place. And not only me. Dennis's DIY, Patel's minimarket, the launderette and the hairstylist. Five working businesses and you undermined them, shut them down for you own ends, and I do mean ends."

Queenan made a weak attempt to fight back. "I did nothing of the kind. That parade was a shambles. It had been for years, and the best thing that could have happened was demolition."

"They were good businesses; they kept people in work, they—"

"Gentlemen, please," Denise interrupted. "There's no point raking up an old argument. It's over, it's done with. Let's concentrate on what we need to know. Mr Queenan, tell us about Vaughan."

"Well, the fact is, I'm, er…"

"Gay?" Joe demanded.

"No. Not gay, but, er…"

"Both sides of the fence?" Denise suggested, and when he looked blankly at her, she added, "AC-DC." When that too fell upon apparently deaf ears, she said, "Bisexual?"

He nodded. "Yes."

"Does you wife know?" Joe asked. He was finding the conversation as uncomfortable as Queenan.

"Good lord, no. I was – am – very discreet."

"So how did Vaughan find out?"

"He saw me at a hotel some years ago. I used this hotel frequently."

"I didn't know we had any gay rendezvous in Sanford?" Joe grumbled.

"It's not in Sanford. It's between York and Beverley."

A light lit In Joe's brain. "Not the Palmer is it?"

"Well, yes it is as a matter of fact. It's not a gay rendezvous, either. They simply ask no questions when you check in. I used it, so did Vaughan and if you know the place, Joe, you'll know it's out in the sticks. Well, Vaughan saw me there one weekend. A few weeks after that, he invited me to one of his parties."

"And you accepted?" Denise demanded. "Even though one of his projects was going through planning?"

"This was four or five years ago," Queenan argued, "And he had nothing going through planning at that time. At least not in Sanford, he didn't. There was absolutely no reason why I shouldn't go." Queenan's face fell. "Of course, later on, when he was seeking planning permission for Britannia Parade…Well, then I wish hadn't gone. In fact, I wished I'd never set eyes on him."

"Blackmail?" Dennis asked.

"In the nicest possible way," Queenan replied with a sad nod. "He had photographs, even a video. Told me he needed my help and if he didn't get it, these images would go to the press and all over the web."

"But you're a local government officer," Joe protested. "You were duty bound to remain impartial."

"I told him that, but he explained how I could persuade the committee without actually appearing to persuade them." Queenan's face fell. "And as you know, it went well until we came up against you." Now his features took on an accusatory appearance, to match his words. "You got me hauled over the coals."

Joe shook his head. "I did nothing of the kind. I fought my corner. I fought for myself and my employees. You dropped yourself in it, Queenan, by giving him the opportunity to get one over on you. Anyway, you objected to Les Tanner and he was replaced as chair of the disciplinary hearing by Kenny Pemberton, and he let you off with a slap on the wrist."

Queenan shuffled uncomfortably in his chair and Joe's mind went into overdrive.

"So you had something on Pemberton, did you? Was he one of Vaughan's regular partygoers, too?"

Queenan gave the barest of nods.

"Men or women?" Denise asked.

"Women," Queenan replied. "At least, I've only ever

seen him with women."

"Oh boy." Joe shook his head in mock humour. "Vaughan had half the damn Town Hall in his pocket."

"That's not fair, Joe," Queenan clamoured. "Like me, Kenny only ever wanted what was best for this town."

"Saving his own arse by helping you save yours? I don't think the cops will look at it quite so leniently."

Horror spread across Queenan's flushed face. "You can't go to the police with this."

"As long as I'm suspected of murder, I can do as I damn well please," Joe snapped. "Right now, Ray Dockerty is short of real suspects, and I can give him two. You and Pemberton. You both had perfect reasons for killing Vaughan, and whatever incriminating evidence he had against you both, was probably kept in his safe or on his computer. And in case you haven't been told, the safe was emptied and the hard drive was taken from the computer. Whoever killed him has it all now."

"I didn't kill him," Queenan pleaded. "And I'm sure Kenny didn't either."

"Even if we believe you, you're still in deep doo-doo," Denise said. "As Joe has just pointed out, the goods Vaughan had on you have disappeared. How long before the killer comes calling and demands cash?"

"And you know something?" Joe smiled viciously. "It couldn't happen to two more deserving people."

Queenan buried his head in his hands. "I'm ruined."

"You will be if you don't co-operate," Denise pointed out. "We're not interested in you and your peccadilloes. We want to know who burned down the old Lazy Luncheonette, and who murdered Vaughan."

"And I don't know the answer to either question. When the old place caught fire, I was worried. When the Fire Service said it had been, er…"

"Torched?"

"Yes. I was in a state of panic. I rang Vaughan and he assured me he had nothing to do with it. He was in Blackpool chasing you at the time, Joe."

"And it never occurred to you that he had the kind of financial clout to pay someone to set fire to the place?"

"Well, yes, of course it did, but he assured me it was nothing to do with him. He wanted the place down, yes, he wanted you out, yes, but he would not go to such extreme lengths."

Denise's eyes widened. "A man blackmailing you and you believed him?"

Listening to Denise, Joe gathered from her tone that she did not believe Queenan.

Queenan's shoulders sagged. "What choice did I have?"

"You could have gone to the police," Denise insisted. "Told them everything. Man up. Show a little courage. Own up to your idiosyncrasies, none of which are illegal, and told them everything. At least they would have stopped Vaughan. You might even have saved his life."

"I couldn't. My marriage... my job... my reputation, all —"

"Mattered to you more than your own corruption and the crimes taking place round you," Joe interrupted. "You disgust me." His anger began to take over. The thought of having spent days in jail because of this man and the shady people who had a hold over him, rattled Joe to the core. "Even now, all you give a damn about is you. You don't care a toss about my reputation, you don't give a hoot about Vaughan, who should be in prison, not dead, you don't care one damn about the run-around you've created for the cops." He made to stand up. "If I ever see you again, Queenan, it'll be too soon."

Joe stood and Denise joined him.

From the other side of the desk, Queenan eyed them timidly. "Will you... will the police have to learn about all this?"

"That, Mr Queenan, depends on how germane it is to Vaughan's death. You should call them and tell them yourself, but I doubt that you will. From our point of view, we offer no guarantees. If we need to tell Superintendent Dockerty, we will."

"And in the meantime," Joe said, "get onto Kenny Pemberton and tell him to expect us."

Queenan sheepishly checked the calendar. "He's not at work. You'll find him either at the magistrates' court, or on the golf course."

***

They paid a quick call into the magistrates' court where they learned that Pemberton had already left for the day, and after that, Joe and Denise drove out to South Sanford Golf Club, an eighteen-hole, former municipal course, not far from the main motorway junction.

"Not my game," Joe said when Denise asked. "I don't mind watching the big tournaments, like The Open, but I can think of better ways of passing the time than knocking a ball three or four hundred yards across open grass."

"My feelings precisely," Denise agreed as they entered the clubhouse. "A lot of the cops played, you know. Spent half their time off walking round the local courses, and I could never understand why. I mean, if they brought the hole a bit nearer, they could get round quicker, couldn't they?"

"Like snooker?"

"Like snooker."

Formerly owned by Sanford Borough Council, now in private hands, the clubhouse was still less appealing than functional, but the new owners had put down a carpet in the main bar.

"An improvement on the composition floor tiles they used to have," Joe said as he approached the bar.

He was told that Pemberton had been on the course for three hours and although no one was quite sure which of the eighteen holes he was playing, he was expected back within the next two hours.

"We'll wait," Joe assured the barman. "In the meantime, give us a half of bitter and a glass of lager."

"You're not members, sir," the barman replied.

This prompted another argument which ended only when Joe demanded to speak to the steward. Like many people in Sanford, Joe had known Vic Yearsley for over forty years, and the rotund bar manager greeted them with a broad smile.

"I'll sign Joe and his lady-friend in as guests," Yearsley told the barman, "and you make sure they're treated accordingly."

"Yes, Mr Yearsley."

"Thanks, Vic."

"So, what are you doing here, Joe? Not thinking of joining are you?"

Joe grunted. "I just told Denise how much I enjoy golf. Watching it, that is. Hey, talking of joining things, how come we haven't seen you applying for the Sanford 3rd Age Club?"

"I don't think I could keep up with that gang of thugs you hang around with, Joe. Besides, the missus has only just agreed to me being in the same town as Brenda Jump, never mind the same bar."

"Poor Brenda," Denise commented as they took their drinks outside and sat on the south-facing terrace to soak up the sun.

"She has a shabby reputation," Joe agreed, "especially among people who don't understand her. But despite what they say, she's no pushover and she's not a bedhopper. After what happened to her husband – cancer, you know – she knows how fragile life is, and she's determined to enjoy every minute of it while she can."

"But she does have a string of boyfriends."

"No," Joe corrected. "She has on-off relationships with one or two men. That's all. And it's more to do with wining and dining than sex. I'll tell you this, Denise. If you needed a friend, an ally, Brenda is the perfect candidate. Not only is she loyal, but she can be as hard as nails when she wants, and she has kick like a donkey." He chuckled. "Vaughan's hard men found that out in Blackpool."

"I like to hear it, but I wasn't, er, having a go at Brenda. I was simply trying to work out where you and she are at."

"We're not at anywhere," Joe replied, taking out his phone. "We had a bit of a fling a year or so back, but it fizzled out. We're good friends, she's an excellent employee and a valuable asset to the 3rd Age Club. But there's nothing beyond that. Not anymore."

"Good."

Joe sensed that Denise was more than happy with his explanation. "I just need to make a phone call."

Searching through the directory, he came to the number for the Palmer Hotel and punched the green button.

"Good afternoon, Palmer Hotel. How may I help you?"

The stock, almost robotic opening irritated Joe. "Let me speak to Yvonne Naylor, please. Tell her it's Joe Murray."

There was a long pause before Yvonne's voice came through. "Hello, Joe. What a pleasant surprise."

"You may think differently in a few minutes," Joe replied. "How are you, Yvonne?"

"I'm very well, thank you. And it's not Mrs Naylor any longer. It's Mrs Vallance. Geoff and I married last summer."

Joe smiled broadly. "Well congratulations. What happened to my invite?"

Yvonne laughed. "We were thinking of inviting you, but we heard that you wouldn't fancy flying to the Seychelles."

"Sounds about right."

"So come on, Joe. What can I do for you?"

"You can tell me all about Gerard Vaughan."

"Oh. Him." Yvonne's disapproval reverberated through the phone, and Joe could imagine her scowl. "You know I can't tell you anything. Client confidentiality and all that, but off the record, I'd have sent him packing to other hotels. Company policy forbade me. Is he causing you trouble?"

"He's dead. Murdered."

"Oh, my God."

"But, yes he's causing me trouble because half the town thinks I did it. I'm not asking for any dirty washing, Yvonne, but I need to find out who really killed him. It's the only way I can get myself off the hook. Can you point me at anyone in particular who he visited at your place?"

"Off the record, and if anyone asks, I'll deny I ever said it. Remember the MP who was murdered while you were here?"

"Edgar Prudhoe? I remember him."

"Try looking at the man who replaced him."

"Hmm." Joe raked his memory. "I don't recall Prudhoe holding a cabinet post."

"I mean in his constituency."

"Oh. Right. Thanks. That all?"

"I could mention one or two others, but they're Sanford born and bred, and, I think, members or employees of your local authority."

"Forget them," Joe suggested. "We're already onto them. Thanks, Yvonne. Give my best to Geoff."

"I will, and thanks for calling, Joe. You know there's always a room for you here."

Joe ended the call, and tossed the phone on the table. Taking a sip of his beer, he said, "We may have problems. Gerard had a big connection. One who might just be desperate enough to kill him."

"Politician?"

"Yep. According to my contact, at least. We need to get on the web, find out where Edgar Prudhoe was the MP. Whoever took the seat over was a *friend* of Vaughan's." Joe placed just enough stress on the word 'friend' for Denise to understand him.

And she promptly disagreed. "Joe, you may not like our elected representatives, but even those with secrets wouldn't resort to murder. Anyway, how would he know to dress it up so it looked like you?"

"All true, but someone like that might just pay a third party to do the job for them. Just the way Vaughan paid someone to torch The Lazy Luncheonette."

Denise drummed her fingers on the table. "We should go to Ray Dockerty with all this."

He dismissed the idea with a growl. "Bloody coppers. They couldn't detect a smell in a bunged up khasi."

Denise chuckled. "Why do you have such a downer on them, Joe?"

"Isn't being accused of murder enough?"

"According to my information, you've been like it most of your life."

"They miss things which, as far as I'm concerned, are obvious," Joe argued. "Yet they concentrate on lines of inquiry which are at best, circumstantial. It's the precise reason I ended up in Sanford nick for four days. Dockerty could not place me at the scene of the crime, and the evidence he had could easily have been cooked up. Hell, he can't even find a motive for me to kill Vaughan. Yet, with a little digging, in the space of a single day, we've come up with a string of motives and at least three other suspects."

"Ray would get there eventually, Joe. I know him. He's a good detective."

"Yes, he probably would, but if it hadn't been for you using your eyes and a little common sense, just as I've been talking about, how much longer would I have sat in that prison cell?"

"There are procedures. Ray was following them. I know, I know, it's bad luck on you, but he didn't put a foot out of place. And it wasn't him who walled you up."

Joe stared across at the eighteenth green where Kenny Pemberton had just arrived. "No, it wasn't. But the clown who did is right there."

It took Pemberton four putts to drop the ball, while his opponent took the hole in three, and the two men came off the green, smiling, laughing and joking, towing their golf trolleys behind them, deep in conversation. It was only when they reached the steps to the clubhouse that Pemberton saw Joe, and the smile left his face.

"I don't know why you're here, Murray, but as a sitting magistrate, moreover, one who remanded you in custody, I can't speak to you."

"I know," Joe admitted. "But you can speak to Denise, and frankly you'd better speak to Denise."

"That sounded like a threat to me. You heard it, didn't

159

you, Norman?"

Pemberton's playing partner nodded, and the Head of Environmental Health turned smugly on Joe.

"You see? I have a witness. Now go away before I call the police."

Joe slid his mobile across the table, "Here, Kenny. Use my phone. You'll find Dockerty's number in the directory somewhere." He sat back and relaxed. "And while he's here we can have a good, long chinwag about those little soirees at Vaughan's place. All right?" Sitting forward he aimed an accusing finger at Pemberton. "And before you start up with your lies, we spent an hour with Irwin Queenan this morning. We know everything, and the only reason we came here instead of going to Dockerty was as a courtesy. We'd like to hear your version."

Pemberton's colour drained. Fastening a fixed, false smile on his face, he addressed his partner. "Sorry, Norman, but it looks like I have business to discuss with this lady. Get your drink and tell the steward to put it on my account."

With a puzzled nod, Norman disappeared into the clubhouse. Pemberton watched him until he was well out of earshot, then rounded angrily on Joe and Denise.

"You listen to me you little—"

Joe cut him off. "Right now you're clinging onto your job, your reputation, possibly your marriage, and even your membership of this club, by the slenderest of threads, and we have the scissors to cut that thread… if we so choose. So sit down and drop the threats. You're in no position to hassle."

Joe waited for Pemberton to obey before going on.

"We know how Vaughan pressured Queenan to get planning permission for Britannia Parade. We know how Queenan pressured you to go easy on him at the disciplinary hearings. We know you frequented Vaughan's parties, but we're not sure whether you were cavorting with boys or girls, or both. What we don't know, but we're sure the police will find out, is how far Vaughan's blackmail went with you."

160

Denise picked up the discourse. "As an ex-police officer, what I know, Mr Pemberton, is that when Joe was brought to court, you never mentioned any relationship with the dead man, although it's clear you had one, and because of that, you should have stood down, not given Joe the opportunity to ask for you to be removed." She smiled, mock-sweetly. "It's the kind of thing a good defence barrister would make a meal of, and guess who would carry the can for it?"

"I followed procedures on the advice of the clerk of the court," Pemberton hissed.

"But the clerk of the court didn't know you used to whoop it up at the dead man's parties, did she?" Joe insisted. "All in all, Kenny, I reckon by the time Dockerty is finished with you, you're probably looking at five years."

The big man's colour drained even further. "I can't go to jail."

"I didn't think I could," Joe reminded him, "but I ended up there last week. You sent me there."

Pemberton was beaten. Like Queenan before him, he capitulated with sagging shoulders and a bowed head. "What do you want?"

"Where were you last Monday night?" Denise asked.

"At home. My wife can verify that. I had nothing to do with his murder."

"How much evidence did Vaughan have against you?"

"Plenty. Photographs, even a video. Just as he had with Irwin."

"And what was the price of his silence?" Joe demanded.

"We go easy on him over environmental issues." Some of Pemberton's fire returned. "I tell you now, there's nothing wrong with that building. It is environmentally sound. It's just that when our boys went in, they weren't as thorough as they usually are, and if they spotted anything, rather than pressing charges, they cut Vaughan some slack. Allowed him time to deal with it."

Joe fumed. "You know, I've spent half my working life fighting with you and your men. You've hassled the hell out

161

of me for dumping fat where I shouldn't, not recycling the stuff I should be recycling, not compartmentalising different environmental hazards. You've dragged me into court no end of times, and when it all turns out, you and Queenan are bigger crooks than me and every other café owner in Sanford."

"You don't understand, Joe. I do my job to the best of my ability, and my concern is for the town. We needed that building."

"It was built by a crook and passed as tickety-boo by another pair of crooks. We can't pick and choose which laws we obey. The rules are laid down, and you're paid to make sure everyone follows them. Not just me and Sid Snetterton, but all of us, and that includes you, Gerard Vaughan and Irwin Queenan."

"So you're saying I should have brought it all out into the open? Let my wife and the whole of the Town Hall find out what I get up to?"

"It's likely to come out anyway, Mr Pemberton." Denise told him. "Right now, Ray Dockerty is short of suspects. Joe is all but cleared, so they'll begin to delve into Vaughan's history. Your name is bound to come up sometime."

A glimmer of confidence appeared in Pemberton's eyes. "As I understand it, all his records, including the hard drive on his laptop, are gone. Up in smoke."

"Then you understand it wrong," Joe told him, and took some satisfaction from the alarm which quickly replaced Pemberton's confidence. "The records are gone, sure. So is the computer hard drive. But they didn't go up in smoke. Vaughan's killer took them, which means that if it isn't you, the killer has everything on you. And he's not likely to want the help of Environmental Health. He's more likely to want every penny in your bank account."

Joe stood up, ready to leave, and glowered down at the slobbering, beaten man.

"When they send you down, ask for Sanford nick. As prisons go, it's pretty comfortable."

Chapter Fourteen

Sitting in Denise's car after leaving the clubhouse, Joe wound down the window to let in some hot, yet fresh summer air.

"We have to take all this to Dockerty," Denise said.

"I know, but I'd rather not. At least not until we get closer to the killer. Something like this could panic him into doing either a runner or something stupid."

"Joe, we're uncovering corruption. If we don't report it, then we're guilty of withholding information. You know what Ray said. If we turn up anything, it has to go straight to him."

Joe seethed in frustration. "I just don't like the idea of him getting away."

"Him?" Denise sound surprised. "You're sure it's a he?"

"Dockerty was."

"But he doesn't know what we know. What about the women Vaughan paid to entertain these men? You're sure it's not one of them who got short-changed?"

"It has to be someone near to me. Someone who knew me well enough to frame me."

"Or someone who could pay a local yokel. There are just too many people for us to go after, now. We have to hand it back to Dockerty."

Fuming in silence, Joe watched her fiddle with the key getting it into the ignition, and the connection snapped in is mind.

"The keys."

"We know how he got the key, Joe. He stole it from your café."

"Keys-z-z-z," Joe said. "Plural. As in more than one of.

Yes, we know how he got the car key, but how did he get the key for the outside cupboard?"

About to start the car, Denise paused. "He didn't. He cut it off with a bolt cutter."

"The padlock, yes, but there's a second lock on that door. An ordinary lock. He needed a key for that. How did he get it? There are only three. I have one, Lee has one and the third is hanging on the rack in The Lazy Luncheonette. He couldn't steal that because we'd have noticed it instantly. So how did he get it?"

Denise fired the engine and slipped the car into reverse. Looking over shoulder to reverse out of the parking space, she said, "You're sure building security don't have one?"

"They may. You think it's one of them?"

"The only alternative is someone stole their key or, more likely, made a plaster cast of it, then had one cut."

She dropped the car into first and pulled away along the gravel drive towards the main Sanford road.

"Well look, before we go rushing to Dockerty with all this, stop in at The Lazy Luncheonette and let's speak to security."

Joe could see the doubt on her face.

"Come on, Denise. It'll only take a few minutes and we may have even more to tell your CID chums."

"All right. You've persuaded me. Which way."

"Turn right and we're a mile up on the right, but you'll have to go past and double back at the roundabout."

But when they got there, Todd Henshaw was adamant that it could not have happened.

Opening the key cupboard, he gestured at the plethora of keys hanging there. "We can get into any place in the building, including your café, Joe. We have to have access in case of fire or any other emergency. But—" He stressed the word, "The keys have to be booked out."

Returning to his station where he could watch the various camera feeds from around the building, he opened the top drawer of the desk, and took out a hardbound, A4 notebook. Many of its pages were full, and each page was divided into

164

columns listing key numbers, time out, signature, time in, signature, reason for taking the key.

"Most of them are general keys," Henshaw went on. "For meter cupboards, electrical control boards, storage areas which the cleaners need access to. Your outside cupboard is key number twenty-two."

He backed up several pages, before the start of the month, and ran his finger carefully down the column of key numbers.

Looking over his shoulder, tracking the numbers with his eye, Joe could see, long before Henshaw got to the end, that Key 22 had never been taken out.

"The only possibility, Joe, is that one of the security staff took it, but I can't see it. We're always double-manned, as you know, and there's the danger that his partner could have noticed. Besides, the bod on that CCTV looks too tall to be one of us."

"Doesn't rule any of you out," Joe told him. "You could have sold it on. But thanks, Todd."

Ten minutes later, they sat at table five in The Lazy Luncheonette where Sheila and Brenda were in mufti after the lunchtime rush. Lee had already gone home, and the two women were cruising down to closing time.

"One of the security men could have taken the key and made a cast for it, then passed it on to the killer," Joe told them after Denise had recounted their day's trial. "Or the killer could have taken it from here and made a cast of it."

"Who would have access to it here, Joe?" Sheila asked. "We'd have noticed."

"Would we?" Joe reached behind him and gathered up several chocolate bars from the counter. Tossing them on the table, he began to unwrap one. "Help yourselves," he invited them. "Just imagine we're in the middle of a rush and the recycling mob call. They come in through the back door and take the key. They've done it enough times in the past. Then there's the Fire Service, Vaughan himself when he came nosying round, and there's probably a hundred and one others who could have lifted the key for a few minutes, made an impression of it, and then put it back."

"Well, I don't recall anyone anywhere near the keys," Brenda said. "Not for weeks. Months maybe. And does it all matter, Joe? After everything you and Denise have learned, you're in the clear."

"But I'm not," he protested, "and that's what's so galling. I'm putting forward alternatives, but if Dockerty cannot place me at Vaughan's or here, then the same is true of all these other possibilities. There's not one shred of evidence to convict them or clear me, and on that basis, I'll still be under suspicion. Am I right, Denise?"

Chewing on chocolate, she nodded gravely, and then swallowed the sweet. "I'm afraid so. I don't believe Dockerty suspects Joe, but because there's a multitude of evidence pointing at him, Ray has no choice but to keep him under suspicion."

"But the video," Brenda cried. "You said it couldn't possibly be Joe."

"And it wasn't," Denise assured her. "But how do we know that Joe didn't pay this man to plant the empty drum? You see? They don't have enough to convict Joe, but they can't clear him either. He remains a suspect. If Ray didn't play it that way, he'd be failing in his duty, and he'd be called to account by his superiors." Denise checked her watch. "And talking of Ray Dockerty, Joe, it's nearly three o'clock and time we were getting to Gale Street."

"One last call before we go there," Joe insisted. "Let's try Frank Utters again."

"Who?"

"Utters the Cutters," Sheila translated. "The heel and key man in the market."

"Oh him. The one who told me he'd cut a car key for you, Joe. Would he do anything so hooky as cutting a key from a mould?"

"Frank's like most traders in this town. They'll do whatever they can to earn a crust."

Market day in Sanford was Wednesday, but the indoor market hall, close to The Gallery shopping mall, was open

166

six days a week. As on any Monday, shoppers were thin on the ground.

"It's worse tomorrow," Joe told Denise as they made their way along the different aisles to the top corner and Utters' stall. "This town is dead as a dodo every Tuesday."

When they got to Utters, they found Frank taking his ease over a cup of tea while studying form on the racing pages of the *Sanford Gazette*. Joe confronted him, but Utters was reluctant to commit at first.

"Cutting keys from a mould is illegal, Joe," he complained.

"Why do you think we came to you?" Joe retorted. "Come on, Frank, you know me, and I know you. As long as it's a paying customer you don't care much what they want."

Utters clucked. "How come I've got a worse reputation than you and I never murdered anyone."

"Neither did I. Now, come on. Let's hear it."

The key cutter sighed. "Yeah, all right. I did one. About three weeks ago."

"Can you describe the man?" Denise asked.

"Man? It was a woman."

Denise hid her surprise. Joe did not.

"A woman?"

"Yeah. Thirty-ish, blonde. Quite, er, tasty if you know what I mean."

"I think I can remember," Joe replied. "So how did she explain needing the key cut from a mould?"

"Reckoned one of her brats kept losing it, or flushing it down the lavatory or whatever. I don't ask questions, Joe. As long as it's not a front door key, I'll do it, and this wasn't a front door key. More like an outside cupboard, if you want my opinion."

Joe dug into his pockets and came out with his bunch of keys. Sorting through them, he held the bunch up by the recycling shed key. "Like this?"

Utters nodded. "Exactly like that. Listen, Joe, you're not going to plod with this, are you?"

"Some of it, "Joe admitted, "but don't worry, Frank. No names, no pack drill."

It was a short walk from the market hall to the police station, where, after being asked to wait because Superintendent Dockerty was in conference with his senior detectives, they were eventually admitted to his office.

Dockerty did not appear to be in the best of moods, but he still greeted them with a barbed joke. "Here they are, look, Ideal Homes and Doctor Washed Pots."

Joe scowled. "Have you ever thought of becoming a comedian, Dockerty? If so, take my advice and stick to directing traffic."

"What do you want? As you can see, we're busy getting nowhere."

Over the next twenty minutes they brought him up to speed about the things they had learned during the day. Dockerty listened intently, but Joe noticed Gemma and Barrett exchanged the occasional awed glance.

When they were through, Dockerty said, "Dare I ask how you came by most of the information?"

"PACE," Denise said with a broad smile.

Even Joe frowned. "PACE?"

"Police and Criminal Evidence Act," Denise explained, and then to Dockerty she said, "We ignored it." She leaned forward resting her elbows on the superintendent's desk and cupping her chin in her hands. "Let's face it, Ray, if you'd spoken to these people, they'd have had lawyers crawling all over you. All we did was apply a bit of, er, pressure."

"None of it will stand up in court without formal investigations, sir," Barrett pointed out.

"I don't need you to tell me that, Ike. However, the information Denise and Joe have brought does permit us to question these people, with or without lawyers. And if you're right, Denise, Joe, about the killer having taken all of Vaughan's information, then the victims are sure to be blackmailed." To his junior officers, he went on, "Full team briefing first thing tomorrow. Ike, get onto Leeds, we may need more bodies. Gemma, speak to Vickers in Wakefield, tell him we might have to call on him for manpower, and while you're at it, track down this MP and then get onto his local force. If he's not at home, talk to the Met. Someone needs to speak to him if only so he can arrange a little damage limitation."

Joe grunted. "Blooming typical. Nobody gives a hoot about my reputation, but because he's an MP he gets the chance to realise his assets and scarper to Brazil before it all hits the fan."

"He'd be wasting his time then," Dockerty riposted. "We've had an extradition treaty with Brazil since the late nineteen nineties." His face became more serious. "I'm sorry about this, Joe, but unfortunately, I still cannot rule you out as a suspect. I believe you're completely innocent, but if I strike you from the list, people above me will be asking why."

Joe glanced sourly at Denise. "That's already been made clear to me." He turned to Gemma. "Have you turned up anything at all?"

"Only Vaughan's naughty parties," she replied. "We spoke to the neighbour, Spencer. He had a moan about you two, and then told us what he'd told you. We were about to begin investigating who might have attended. Looks like we don't have to bother now."

In what appeared to Joe as an effort to re-establish control over proceedings, Dockerty ordered, "I want informal interviews with these people at the Town Hall. Particularly Pemberton. With his links to Vaughan, there is no way he could sit on that bench. Use the threat of charges as a lever." He turned a more benign eye on Joe. "By the way, we owe you a vote of thanks."

"Makes a change. What have I done to deserve such praise."

"Eric Neave."

"Who... oh, the silly old duffer I shared a cell with."

"The very man. When you told me about his azalea bush, I got onto Leeds, and they lifted it out of the planter. They found the knife which was used to murder Neave's wife.

Enough DNA on it to start our own laboratory, but we found traces of the neighbour on it. Neave had been saying he was innocent all along. Looks like he was telling the truth."

"Hmm." Joe shook his head. "You're sure he didn't pay the neighbour to get rid of his wife? From all I heard, Neave and his missus didn't enjoy the friendliest of relationships."

"The neighbour is being questioned." With that, Dockerty turned back to his two officers to continue the briefing.

Joe switched off. In front of him on the desk was a buff folder from which the edge of a large photograph projected. He opened the folder and found himself staring at an image of Vaughan's badly charred body.

Frowning in disgust, he shuffled it to the back and did the same with two more shots of the body taken further away and from different angles. While the chatter continued around him he next looked at a picture of Vaughan's laptop, melted and charred, its back open where the hard drive had been removed. Next was an image of Lee's kitchen knife, its once shiny blade now blackened, but the initials L.M. standing out clearly on the burned handle.

Joe recalled the day, almost fifteen years ago, when he gave the set to the young Lee.

"You make sure no one nicks 'em, lad," he had said. "I know what those thieving sods at the college are like."

"No worries, Uncle Joe. Anyone tries and I'll paste 'em."

Joe had disapproved of the threat, but replied more logically. "You have to be able to identify them, you idiot. Put some kind of mark on them so you know they're yours."

Lee had spent most of the day using a nail and his raw strength to carve initials into the handles so deeply that even the ravages of two fires would not erase them.

Joe shuffled the photograph to the back and found himself looking at an image of the pen. Once again, it was blackened and charred, the fine matte silver coating burned off, tossed incongruously on the floor, as if it had fallen there. The image evoked memories of the day Alec Staines had brought it into The Lazy Luncheonette.

The week previously Joe had cleared up a murder in Windermere, and exonerated Alec's son, Wes. But he was loath to accept the pen.

"I was only doing what I always do."

"You got Wes off the hook, and Julia was pretty snappy with you at one bit. It's a bit of summat and nowt, Joe, but it's just our way of saying thanks."

So he accepted it, but he never used it, and even if he could not see the inscription in the photograph, he could recite it. *To Joe, with thanks. Alec and Julia.*

"Enjoying our album, Joe?"

Joe looked up from the photographs to find Dockerty staring at him.

"It's certainly bringing up some memories, but I wouldn't keep it in the cupboard with my wedding pictures."

Dockerty reached across and closed the folder before taking it back. "As a suspect, you shouldn't even be looking at them."

"What do you think I'm gonna do? Scan them and slot them into my black album? Are we through here, yet?"

"As far as I'm concerned, yes," Dockerty replied. "Thanks. Both of you. You've given us lines of inquiry we can pursue, but I won't kid you, Joe. This could be a long haul."

Joe stood up, Denise followed suit.

"Keep us informed," Joe said as they left.

With Joe leading the way, he and Denise stepped out into the hot sun of five in the afternoon.

"You staying at my place again, or are you going home?" he asked.

"Why? Are you eager to see the back of me, or looking for a bit more, er, action?"

"No, it's not that. I don't have much in the fridge or the freezer. Tell you what. Let's go over to the frozen food shop. Coupla TV dinners, eh?"

"Why not?"

They ambled across the market square, through the stalls,

Joe nodding or saying hello to people he knew, prompting Denise to ask, "How come everyone seems to know you?"

"History," Joe replied. "This is a mining town. At one time, half the population worked at the pit, and the other half ran the businesses which fed off the miners' wages. My old man opened the café just after World War Two, and it's been a fixture on Doncaster Road ever since. Right now, I'm the last of the original Murrays, but Lee has the family name and when he takes over, he'll carry it on. Hopefully, his son, Danny, will follow him."

"Sanford sounds like those remote Scottish islands where everyone knows everyone else."

"Similar," Joe agreed. "But in our case it's coal, not fishing, sheep or cattle farming that binds the community." He frowned as they entered the frozen food shop. "I never thought it was a bad thing. Community. You know. But they're falling apart fast these days."

"Middle age, Joe. It's catching up with you."

The shop, like most others, was almost empty. At the two checkouts, attendants appeared bored, ready to knock off and go home. Joe purposely did not rush, but hurried Denise along when she opened the lid of a ready meals cabinet and suggested a chicken and mushroom risotto.

"Not fond of Italian," he told her, and lifted the next lid, from where he took out a frozen dinner for one of roast beef and Yorkshire pudding.

"Good for me," she told him.

"You might find the beef is a bit bland," Joe said, turning the carton on its side to study the cooking instructions. "It always is with these frozen things."

Screwing up his eyes, he held the carton at arms' length, then close up, then even closer, then at arms' length again.

"I think it's time I was getting reading glasses," he muttered. "Either that, or they should print the instructions a bit larger."

Denise laughed, took it from him and turned it over. "You're trying to read it upside down, you barmpot."

Joe grinned and took the box from her again. And as he

began to read, his eyes widened. A look of realisation spread across his tanned features.

"Upside down. Of course. That's it."

"What?" Denise asked. "You're going to turn it over in the microwave?"

"What? Come again? No, not the bloody dinner." His eyes burned into her. "Denise, I know who did it. I know who murdered Vaughan."

Chapter Fifteen

It was a nervous Joe who answered the door.

On the journey from Sanford town centre to Joe's flat, Denise had repeatedly asked if he was sure of his facts, and Joe repeatedly explained how he came by his conclusion.

"But I have no proof, and if we give it to Ray Dockerty, it'll lead to a series of interviews and a string of denials. There are any number of explanations and they'll come streaming out. We need a confession."

"And how do you propose we get one?"

It was a problem that dogged Joe as he chewed through the bland, largely tasteless TV dinner. Sat at the table under the open window, the fresh, summer air carried in on a light breeze did nothing to lift his spirits. It might just as well be the depths of winter.

"It's risky," he explained while they washed, dried and put away the dishes. "He's a big bugger, and I guarantee he won't be alone, but if we can get him out here, and record everything, we're in with a shout."

"Record it how?" Denise asked.

Joe held up his smartphone. "This has a voice recording app."

"Test it," Denise instructed.

Activating the application, Joe placed the phone on the windowsill and pulled the curtain across an inch or two to hide it.

Coming away from it, to the middle of the room, he said, "Mary had a little lamb its fleece was white as snow. Mary went up the hill with Jack and Jill, eating kebabs on the go."

Denise did not find it remotely amusing and when they played it back, although it was audible, it was difficult to hear. Even running the recording through Joe's computer made it only slightly clearer.

"The police could enhance it," Denise agreed. "But our man is likely to suspect something like this Joe."

"No sweat," he said, and brought out his netbook. "This has an inbuilt webcam. He'll probably spot it and shut it down. That should make him feel safe."

Denise chewed her lip. "I'd be much happier if we brought Dockerty in on this."

"He'll screw it up."

"You mean you want to show him how much smarter you are."

"By not screwing it up." Joe nodded. "Come on, Denise. You're an ex-cop. You know how to look after yourself."

"Yes, but when I was a cop, I usually had backup, and according to everyone, when it comes to fighting, you're as much use as a chocolate teapot." She made an effort to seriously stress her worries. "Dockerty warned us about him on Saturday, Joe, and I have no reason to disagree with Ray. This man has killed once. What makes you think he won't kill again? As in kill us?"

"I think he may have killed Vaughan in the heat of the moment. I don't see him as a serial nutter. Trust me, Denise, I know this man. I've known him years."

"Yes, and he still murdered Vaughan – assuming you have it right, so that shows you how well you really knew him."

"Yes, but if you phone Dockerty, he'll tell you not to do it, and that gives our man the chance to dream up even more excuses. Denise, our only chance is a confession. We have to pin him down or he'll get away with it."

"Could we not call Sheila or Brenda and tell them to keep the line open so they can overhear?"

"Well, we could, but they're more technologically backward than me, so there's no guarantee the line would stay open. And they would never get their heads round trying to record it. I don't think I would, come to that. It would be our word against his. We need a confession and

175

we need it recorded. I have to have him here to I can push him."

At that point, she capitulated. "All right. But we keep them between us. That way if they go for either of us, the other is there to intervene."

Joe picked up his phone and dialled.

"It's Joe Murray. You have some explaining to do, and you'd better get over to my place to do it before I call the cops."

There were protests from the other end, but Joe cut off the call without listening to them.

They spent the next twenty minutes setting up the trap, and then watching TV, until the doorbell rang. Joe started the webcam on the netbook, and the voice recorder on his smartphone and hid the phone while leaving the netbook in clear view on the table. Closing the window to avoid giving their man the temptation of leaning over and spotting the phone, as the doorbell rang a second time he took a deep breath and made his way along the hall to answer it.

Brad Kilburn smiled as the door opened. Joe did not. He stood back to let Kilburn in, and allowed Alan Corbin, who was carrying a small hold-all, to follow. Closing the door, Joe led them to the living room, where he risked a glance at the window and the hidden smartphone, praying that the voice recorder was still working.

Joe joined Denise on the settee, picked up the TV remote and witched the set off. Fixing Kilburn's stare, he said, "We know everything."

"Fine," Kilburn replied with a grin. "Can you tell us what's going to win the Ebor Handicap?"

"Funny. Ha-ha. You should be on the telly. You'd look good next to a picture of my folks."

Kilburn's smile disappeared. "Get to the point, Joe, because all this is a mystery to us."

"You made a mistake. You told Gemma that the pen was engraved."

"And it was. Or didn't they show you the photographs?"

"They did, but unfortunately, in the pictures the SOCOs

176

took, the inscription was face down, and you told Gemma that you and your boys hadn't touched the pen. So how did you know about the engraving?"

The fireman shrugged. "So I was wrong. One of my people did move it."

"Shove it, Kilburn," Denise snapped. "You knew because you salvaged that pen from the original fire at the old Lazy Luncheonette."

Kilburn laughed. "Did I?" he turned to his partner. "Sort it, Al."

Much to the puzzlement of Joe and Denise, Corbin disappeared, first into the hall, and when he returned after a few minutes, into the kitchen.

"Sort what?" Joe asked.

"All in good time, pal, all in good time."

Concentrating on the task at hand, Joe said, "What we can't work out is why you waited so long to kill Vaughan. Fifteen months. Why?"

Brimming with confidence, Kilburn said, "I didn't take the pen and the knife with the intention of killing him. I took them to plant on him."

Denise frowned. "Again?"

Kilburn sat at the table and toyed with the keyboard of Joe's netbook. Joe watched him, offering up a silent prayer that he would not spot the smartphone. But Kilburn appeared quite content running his index finger on the mousepad while facing them. Then he stared at the screen and grinned. "Nice try, Joe." He turned to the computer, and shut down the webcam, but to Joe's puzzlement, he made no effort to erase the few minutes of video which had already been taken.

Instead, he spoke directly to them. "When you threatened to appeal the compulsory purchase order, Vaughan asked us to torch your old place. No sweat. We've done it before for other people. He never said how he knew, but I guess one of them told him, and let's face it, when you have a deliberate firing, the last person you think might have fired it is the very man who's risking his life to put it out. This time the

177

payoff was serious. Not a lousy ten grand. Vaughan wanted that building levelled so badly that when I asked for fifty grand, he agreed right away, and paid us ten in advance."

"You're telling me that Vaughan had it planned before we even went to Blackpool?" Joe demanded.

"The week before as a matter of fact," Kilburn replied. "Think about it, Joe. Fifty big ones. You spoke to Fen yesterday, so you know we're on our way to the Middle East. Both Al and me both got a decent payoff, and with the fifty grand Vaughan owed us, we would be set until the money starts coming in. But I didn't trust Vaughan. I found the pen and the knife when I was checking the old building on the morning of the fire, and I decided to keep them. If Vaughan screwed us around, I'd plant them and finger him for the fire. And as it happens, I was right. He did nothing but hedge and hedge and hedge."

"Because he had a hold on you, didn't he?" Joe demanded. "You and Corbin. You're an item."

Kilburn laughed. "Wrong. I'm a married man. So is Al. We knew Vaughan was that way inclined, we knew Queenan liked his fun and games, and we knew Pemberton liked his women, but we never had anything to do with those parties. Mind you, I'm willing to bet that's where he learned about our little sideline in pyromania. His scene wasn't mine, Joe. Obviously, you are right when you say he had a hold on us. Records, Joe. Kept in his safe and on his computer. And amongst them was a video. Secret filming of us agreeing to fire your old place."

"My Mexican standoff," Denise commented.

"Dunno about yours, but you're right. Course, we had more to lose than him. He'd have got, maybe, ten years for his part, but we'd have gone down longer, and our friends in the Middle East would have washed their hands of us before we could even get out there. His trouble was, as I'm sure you remember, he was too sure of himself. He knew we'd started a few fires, but he didn't realise we were prepared to kill if necessary."

Joe was appalled. "Just like that?" He snapped his

fingers.

"If you like. Truth is, he was stringing us along." The fireman stopped playing with the computer and leaned forward, stressing his point. "He did pay us for torching your place, but only the ten grand I mentioned. I spent over a year hassling with him for the other forty and it was one excuse after another. He was a danger to us, too, remember. Put too much pressure on and he might just tell your Gemma or Don Oughton what he knew, even if it meant risking jail. So we decided to get rid of him."

"And cut your losses on the payoff?"

"Again, not entirely. I knew that Vaughan kept a few thou in his safe, along with those written records. I also knew where he kept the key. The documents and the hard drive from the computer came away with us, and the cash went into my bank last Tuesday morning and it's winging its way to the Middle East as we speak."

Corbin returned from the kitchen. "All set, Brad."

"What's all set?"

"You'll find out in a few minutes," Kilburn assured them.

Joe scowled at Corbin. "What size shoes do you take? No. Let me guess. Twelve. Right?"

The younger man laughed. "Plod must have found something, Brad."

"Latent footprint somewhere," Kilburn agreed, before addressing Joe and Denise again. "You've probably guessed I took your car key a coupla weeks back."

"We didn't know it was you until this afternoon," Joe agreed, "But yeah, we knew someone had taken it. You also took casts of the keys for the outside cupboard, didn't you? Then had your wife make a copy."

"Alan's wife as it happens. I couldn't go. Neither could Al, and my missus is fairly well known." Kilburn shook his head good-naturedly. "Never trust anyone with your keys, Joe. Not even the Fire Service. I couldn't steal 'em, obviously. I didn't know if you had a spare set and even if you had, those keys gone with your car key might have aroused your suspicions, and it would have pointed the

179

finger straight at me. But you're lazy. You couldn't be bothered even to come out to the recycling shed with me. So while I was alone, I took an impression while I was out back, then made a plaster mould at home. Al's wife had Frank Utters cut us a key from it. He smiled confidently. I have to say, Joe, we never really expected the charges against you to stick. We just wanted someone to carry the can while we got out of the country."

"Been a bit slow, then, haven't you?" Denise grumbled.

"Well, we did think the cops would take a bit longer about releasing Joe, and if you hadn't poked your nose in, they probably would have. That aside, both Alan and I had to work our notice with the Fire Service. I'm a serving watch manager, I had to give one month's notice." Kilburn grinned again. "It was up last Friday, and as Fen told you, we're on the first plane out of here tomorrow."

"Unless we call the cops," Joe said.

Kilburn laughed good-naturedly. "Funny thing that, Joe. I told Alan you would be alone. I'm certain you haven't spoken to Dockerty, or even your Gemma. Cos you're a little smartarse, aren't you? Like to show just how clever you are alongside the cops. And even if you had called them, so what?" He jerked a thumb back towards the computer. "Now that your little video is shut down, you have no evidence, and I can give Dockerty a thousand reasons why I knew that pen was engraved."

"Tell you what I don't understand. How did your pal here get away with not showing up for the fire at Vaughan's?"

"According to everyone else, he did show up," Kilburn said. "That's the thing about big emergencies, Joe. You're so busy you don't know who's who. You just listen for orders tagged onto your name. I just threw Alan's name in a few times. Everyone else will swear that he was with us." He clapped his hands like a market trader about to make an offer. "So, what happens now? Eh? Where are you gonna go from there?"

"We call the cops." Joe's declaration was more in hope than confidence.

Kilburn laughed again. "Oh no," he said, wagging his finger. "What really happens is Al and I get the hell out of here on the first plane to Amsterdam."

"And of course, we promise not to call the cops for two days so you can pick up your Middle East connection," Denise sneered.

"You wouldn't do that even if I agreed," Kilburn said.

"Stop playing games, Kilburn. So what is happening?"

"Murder, is what's happening, Joe. Again. Only this time there'll be two victims. You and ex-Detective Sergeant Latham, here."

"If you think I'm gonna sit back and let you…" Joe half stood before trailing off and sinking back into his seat as Kilburn drew a taser.

"Nasty little things, you know," the fireman said. "And if you try anything silly, I'll use it on you."

Denise moved, and Kilburn turned it on her.

I told you we should have called Dockerty," Denise grumbled as she sat down again.

With them both tamed again, Kilburn watched Corbin dig into his holdall for rolls of duct tape.

"You know the wonderful thing about being a fireman? It's not just putting fires out. It's learning how to set them, too." He nodded at Corbin. "Tell 'em, Al."

Every bit as cool and confident as his boss, Corbin said, "A bit back, you asked what I was sorting." He held up two disc-shaped lithium batteries. "I took these from your smoke alarms, and obviously, I knocked off the circuit breaker for them at the mains. They won't work at all now." He smiled glibly. "Did you know that hot dishes and ignored cooking hobs are the biggest single cause of fires right across the world? I've put a pan of cooking oil on the gas burner in the kitchen, Joe." Corbin checked his watch. "My guess is it will ignite in about another ten minutes. I'll run more oil everywhere, so it'll spread rapidly. Once we have you and your girlfriend tied to the chairs, we're gonna run a trail to your feet, so you can watch each other burn."

"Assuming the smoke doesn't kill you first, that is,"

Kilburn said.

Joe's heart began to pound. In an effort to hide his fear, he declared, "It doesn't matter what you do, the police will still know it's murder."

"Of course they will," Kilburn agreed. "But why should that lead them to us? After all, we put out the fire at The Lazy Luncheonette, and the one at Vaughan's place and the only evidence against us is yours." Kilburn gestured at the computer. "That'll burn with you two."

Praying that his voice recording was still working, Joe now understood why he had made no effort to erase the short video already on the machine.

Kilburn moved the two dining chairs to the centre of the room facing each other, several feet apart and motioned Joe to take one while Corbin silently ordered Denise to the other. Corbin handed Kilburn a roll of tape and while the younger man began strapping Denise to her chair, Kilburn began work on Joe.

"Hands hanging down, Joe, in line with the chair legs."

"Listen, Kilburn, it's not too late—"

"It is for you, pal." Kilburn began to strap Joe's right hand to the chair leg.

Dredging his memory, Joe recalled online videos he had watched of people escaping from duct tape bindings. He let the heel of his hand rest on the chair leg, while keeping his palm and fingers a millimetre or two away from it. He was afraid, but he had long ago learned that the trick with fear was not to let it dominate you.

Determined to distract Kilburn as much as he could, he said, "There are other people who know most of what we know. You won't get away with it."

"We might, we might not. Either way, you won't be around to know the difference."

Happy that he had secured the right hand and wrist, Kilburn applied himself to the left.

Opposite Joe, Corbin had already strapped Denise's hands to the chair legs, had taped over her mouth, and was now strapping her ankles to the chair.

"You know, Joe, getting out of duct tape isn't all that difficult," Kilburn waffled, "but you need strength to do it, and let's face it, you don't have any. You weigh about three stones wet through and I've seen more muscle on a sausage roll."

"Untie me, then, and let's put it to the test. I'll beat your brains in. Both of you."

Kilburn laughed generously at the nonsensical bravado. "Joe Murray and his gang. I don't remember you from school, but I heard the legend. Joe Murray couldn't fight his way out of a paper bag. It was George Robson and Owen Frickley who did all the scrapping. You were all brain and no brawn."

"You forgot Brenda Jump," Joe said as Kilburn began work on his ankles, strapping them to the chair leg.

He used the same manoeuvre he had with is hands, lifting his heel slightly, but this time Kilburn noticed.

"Feet flat," he ordered.

"I can't, you idiot. I'm too short." Joe made a show of trying to make his foot reach to ground.

Kilburn did not buy it. Grabbing Joe's ankle, he pulled the foot down and flat, and Joe winced.

"When I say feet flat, I mean feet flat." He wrapped tape around Joe's ankle.

"Don't you think you're in enough trouble as it is?"

It was one of those silly, pointless questions, but it was designed to distract Kilburn, not to be taken seriously.

"The sentence for murder is life," Kilburn replied as he strapped Joe's left ankle. "You can only serve one life no matter how many you've shined on."

With his roll of tape running low, he strapped Joe's torso to the chair back, and as he did so, Joe pushed out his chest very slightly. Enough to give him some play when Kilburn and Corbin left.

"Kilburn, I'm begging you one last time—"

"Let's see if this will shut you up." Kilburn tore off the final piece of tape from the roll.

"I'll see you in hell."

"Happen. But you'll get there first." The fireman slapped the tape over Joe's mouth.

As he did so, Joe puckered his lips. He had not shaved since early morning.

With the two victims firmly secured, Kilburn nodded at Corbin who delved into his bag again, and came out with a five-litre can of cooking oil. Uncapping it, and starting by spreading it over Denise's feet, then Joe's, he laid a trail back into the kitchen. He emerged a few moments later and picked up his bag.

"The pan on the hob is bubbling and it won't be long before it starts to smoke, Brad. I reckon no longer than five minutes. I've spread oil on the cooker top and down the front."

"Time to go. See you, Joe, Denise... not." Kilburn laughed and the two men left.

Before the door closed Joe was wriggling in his chair. Kilburn had assumed he had no strength, but it was not entirely true. He had spent his life lifting heavy weights in the kitchen of his café, as a result of which his wiry frame was as supple as it had ever been. Twisting his chest this way and that, straining and twisting both hands he also worked on his left foot. An attempt to twist his right foot proved pointless. It was strapped tight to the chair leg.

He manoeuvred his chair away from the trail of oil, and using his eyes, signalled Denise to do the same. If the oil ignited, the break in the trail would give them an extra few seconds which might make all the difference. Across from him, Denise too began to wriggle, breaking that trail. As he strained against his bonds, Joe silently congratulated her. At least she had understood his silent message.

Working his lips, he felt the tape across his mouth beginning to give against the day's stubble under his nose. Both hands and his chest were freeing up, and his left ankle was making inroads against the bindings.

The tape covering his mouth gave, and he spat it away. Able to talk at last, he said, "I'm going to let the chair fall and see if it snaps the tape."

184

Dennis shook her head as the tape across her mouth also began to give. "If the tape is loose it might not work."

"You fancy frying in here?" he asked, and began to rock his chair from side to side. "I wish I had one of those old slot meters for the gas. At least the shilling might run out before we go up in smoke."

Continuing to strive against the tape, he rocked the chair more and more, gathering impetus as he did so. Denise continued to struggle to free herself. From the kitchen the first wisps of smoke crept into the room at ceiling level.

The chair reached a critical angle, and hovered for a moment. Joe realised it was about to swing back and go the other way. He heaved as far as he could to his right, and the chair toppled.

He hit the carpet with a crack, and he cried out. It was not the tape giving way at his right wrist, but the wrist itself, fracturing under the impact and the pressure of the rigid chair leg to which it was tied.

Denise winced in sympathy and went back to struggling against her bonds.

Pain shot through him and Joe's head spun. He lingered on the verge of unconsciousness, darkness threatened to engulf him.

"JOE," Denise screamed. "STAY WITH ME, JOE."

Her words reached his buzzing ears and sank in. He focussed his attention, shook his head to clear it, and looked up from his sideways prone position. The smoke was getting darker and thicker. A lifetime spent working in kitchens told him they had only a matter of minutes before it ignited. They had to either remove it from the heat source or get out.

The fall had loosened the bindings further at his right wrist. He rolled the chair onto its back, and with the pain bringing tears to his eyes, he worked at the damaged wrist. At the same time, he strained at the other bonds.

Nearby, Denise still struggled, and her bindings were, likewise, giving way. She began to cough as the smoke reached her lungs.

Joe heaved one last time. His wrist protested with lances of agony, but the tape broke. He threw off the chest bindings, reached down to his left ankle and freed it. Then he freed his left wrist.

The tape around his right ankle was still too tight. Desperately trying to ignore the pain, he struggled into an upright position and, dragging the chair with him, made for the kitchen

"There isn't time, Joe," Denise cried. "We have to get out."

"If I can cover the pan with a wet towel, and turn off the gas…"

Joe trailed off. With a loud WHOOSH, the pan in the kitchen ignited and flame rushed upwards and down the front of the cooker, to follow the trail into the living room.

Joe backed off, his arm raised against the wall of heat, and the flames singed the hairs on his forearm. He looked frantically through the blaze into the kitchen and his heart sank. The MDF worktops and cupboards above and to the side of the cooker were already blackening, and soon the heat would reach their flashpoint.

"JOE, GET ME OUT OF THIS!!!"

Denise's screamed reminded him. Still dragging his chair, he hobbled back to her, and began unravelling her bonds. In a matter of seconds, she was free and bent to untie his right ankle from the chair.

As his foot was freed, he leaned across the table, snatched up his netbook and reached to the windowsill for his phone.

"We don't have time, Joe," Denise shouted as the flames began to lick at the living room wallpaper.

"The evidence is on these," he called back. "Now go."

The settee was backed up to the rear wall. A sheet of flame erupted from it and threatened to block their exit.

"That was supposed to be fireproofed," Joe grumbled.

"So sue them," Denise advised.

She raised her arm to ward off the heat and rushed out of the room, into the hall. Joe followed, his trainer, doused in oil, catching light. He slammed the living room door shut behind him. Smoke began to billow from under it. Denise hurried out of the apartment.

Making his way along the hall, he opened the last cupboard door on the left. "Warn the neighbours," he ordered.

"What the hell are you doing?"

He did not answer but stepped into the cupboard.

"Joe, this is no time to think of saving your ironing board."

Again Joe ignored her. Smoke was building up behind him, choking him, blinding him. His wrist hurt, but he clung onto both the phone and the netbook. An old blanket which he had used as a dustsheet when painting the walls, covered the detritus of modern life. Dragging it away, kicking a box of household trivia out of his way, he reached down, gripped the mains gas tap, and yanked it up, cutting off the supply.

He staggered back out of the cupboard. Through the thick smoke, he could see flames now eating away at the hollow, flush door. Pain spoke to him. He looked down and realised his trousers were now singed, and his trainer was ablaze. Reaching into the cupboard, he snatched up the old blanket and smothered his lower leg beneath it. A rush of heat struck him. He looked to the living room but could no longer see the doorway for the flames.

He turned and dashed out of the flat.

Chapter Sixteen

With his wrist temporarily bandaged, and an oxygen mask in place, Joe coughed smoke from his tortured lungs, and stared around at the chaos.

He and Denise had notified his immediate neighbours, and the process of getting everyone out of the building had gathered momentum from there. With people knocking on doors, getting others to safety, Joe had dialled 999 and got the Fire Brigade and police out. After that, he rang Dockerty, only to be put through to Gemma. He told her everything, and she rang off promising to get onto the airport. Almost as an afterthought, he called for an ambulance for himself and Denise.

Neither was badly injured. Smoke had done much of the damage, but Joe had also suffered a fractured wrist and his right leg was a little scorched.

"Which is more than can be said for my trainers," he said, looking glumly on the remains of his right shoe.

Once everyone was out of the building the police had shepherded the tenants to the far end of the car park, where they would be out of harm's way. When the fire engines arrived, the crew went in and thanks to the information Joe and Denise were able to give on the source and accelerant, the blaze was under control in less than an hour, by which time, Gemma and Ike Barrett had arrived with bad news.

"No sign of them at the airport, Uncle Joe," Gemma said. "Are you sure they said the first flight to Amsterdam?"

It was Denise who confirmed it with a nod. Pulling her oxygen mask out of the way, she said, "Kilburn's no fool. He probably realised we had a slight chance of getting out, so he fed us false information. Maybe they're flying from

Manchester, or even Robin Hood."

"Well they've missed the Amsterdam flight from Leeds," Barrett said. "But you do have your, er, evidence intact?"

Joe handed over his smartphone and netbook. "Our findings are on the computer, and there's part of a video on there before Kilburn shut it down. There's a voice recording on the phone. I don't know how good it will be, but Kilburn told us everything. Including how he torched the old Lazy Luncheonette after Vaughan paid him to do it."

Gemma and Ike wandered off to listen to the recording, and Fen Appleton approached them.

"The flat is completely ruined, Joe, and we won't be letting anyone back into the block until tomorrow at the earliest. It needs the building inspectors in to declare it habitable again." He waved at the tenants, crowded on the car park. "Looks like we'll have to open the church hall and get some temporary beds in." He laughed. "Maybe we could get your Lee to man the soup kitchen."

"He has a café to run, Fen," Joe retorted, his voice muffled through the oxygen mask. "You could speak to Sheila Riley and Brenda Jump, though. Ask them to rustle up volunteers from the Sanford 3rd Age Club."

"I'll tell the council wallahs."

Council officers and reporters had not been far behind the emergency services. While both Joe and Denise refused to give an interview, promising the *Gazette* reporters and photographers the exclusive later, Joe spotted Irwin Queenan amongst the council employees, and waved him over to the ambulances.

Removing his oxygen mask, he kept his grime-covered features as neutral as he could. "Word of warning, Queenan. Ray Dockerty knows everything about who did this, and it was the same people as did the old Lazy Luncheonette. They were linked directly to Gerard Vaughan, and they're going to be talking to you and Pemberton. Chances are, it's gonna hit the fan big time, but at least there will be no more blackmail of either of you."

Queenan blanched. "I, er, I'm sorry, Joe. I was protecting

189

myself and my wife, and I never thought matters would get to this point."

"Yes, well, your name is gonna get dragged into it. If I were you, I'd speak to your bosses and your wife now. While you have the chance. Dockerty was going to take you both in tomorrow morning, but he has this lot to deal with." Joe waved at the scene around them. "It'll give you and Pemberton a little breathing space to talk to your families."

Queenan sighed. "I think, maybe you're right."

As he wandered off, the senior paramedic turned her attention on the two patients once more. "We need to get you to the hospital, Joe, and get that wrist properly dressed, and the foot strapped up. And you need to go there, too, Denise. You'll both need chest x-rays and your breathing checked."

As she spoke, Superintendent Dockerty's black Volvo arrived.

"Just give us another few minutes," Joe pleaded. "Let's see what the bigwigs from the police station have to say."

"Five minutes. No longer."

Dockerty climbed out of the driver's seat, and to Joe's cynical surprise, Donald Oughton got out of the nearside.

"What price this is an official deputation apologising for walling me up?"

"You can't claim against them, Joe," Denise said.

"No. But I can make them look like bumbling idiots."

The two senior officers approached Gemma and Ike Barrett and spent a few minutes talking with them, and then all four walked to the ambulance.

"Joe, Denise, we owe both of you a debt of gratitude... again," Oughton said. "And Joe, you have my personal apology for the arrest and, er, subsequent, er—"

"Incarceration?" Denise suggested.

"That can all come later," Joe told them. "What about Kilburn and Corbin? You need to get an all ports warning on them."

"We did," Dockerty said. "The moment Gemma rang me I guessed they might be joshing you, so I put out an APW on them. They were picked up twenty minutes ago on the A63, going through Hull."

Joe smiled for the first time in hours. "North Sea ferry?"

Dockerty nodded. "Overnight to Zeebrugge. According to my opposite number in Humberside, his people say Kilburn and Corbin had a hire car waiting in Zeebrugge and tickets for a flight from Istanbul to Dubai on Wednesday. They're also carrying a lot of cash, and a folder of, as yet, unidentified documents bearing the Gleason Holdings logo, and what looks like a hard drive from a computer. Vaughan's?"

"Opportunities for blackmail, I reckon." Joe grunted at his niece. "Like I told you, Gemma, our findings are all on the netbook." He sighed. "Looks like they were going to make their way overland to Turkey."

"Then fly down to Dubai where they could disappear." Denise shook her head, sadly.

Gemma beamed on her uncle. "We'll have to keep your phone and computer as evidence, Uncle Joe. You won't get them back until after the trial."

Joe smiled wanly at Denise. "The insurance might stand new… again."

The paramedics returned. "Right, you two, no more chitchat. Mask on, Mr Murray. You too, Ms Latham. We're getting you down to the hospital. Get you checked over."

Joe followed Denise into the ambulance. Once seated, the paramedic fastened safety belts around them.

The ambulance moved off. The paramedic seated herself close to the front, where she could converse with her driver through a grille.

Joe voiced his glum thoughts. "I'm homeless. Again. Second time in less than a year and a half."

"Look on the bright side, Joe," Denise encouraged him. "At least you won't have me looking to pin it on you this time. And by the time we're through, I'll pull in a considerable reward for this."

"You will?"

"The insurance company will tackle Vaughan's estate in

an effort to claw back the money they paid you. And they'll pay out again this time, but they'll make an effort to get it back from Kilburn and Corbin."

"If their wives haven't already spent it." Joe clucked. "And it's not going to do my premiums any favours is it? They went through the roof after the last fire, and I can see it happening again… if they're willing to insure me."

Denise chuckled through her mask. "Poor old Joe. Tell you what, do you want to crash at my place until Sanford Council find you somewhere?"

"You don't mind?"

"Course not. But you'd better let the medics help you get your breath back first." Denise grinned. "You're going to need all the energy you can find."

THE END

Fantastic Books
Great Authors

CROOKED
CAT

Meet our authors and discover
our exciting range:

- Gripping Thrillers
- Cosy Mysteries
- Romantic Chick-Lit
- Fascinating Historicals
- Exciting Fantasy
- Young Adult and Children's
  Adventures

Printed in Great Britain
by Amazon